Nathaniel's Place

A novel

By Sinéad Tyrone

NFB
Buffalo, New York

Copyright © 2025 Sinéad Tyrone

Printed in the United States of America

Nathaniel's Place/Tyrone—1st Edition

ISBN: 979-8-9985457-8-8

Fiction
Fiction> Romance
Fiction> Ireland
Fiction> Irish Heritage

This is a work of fiction. All characters are fictitious. Any resemblance to actual events or locations, unless specified, or persons, living or dead is entirely coincidental.

No part of this book may be reproduced or transmitted in any form by any means, electronic or mechanical, including photocopying, recording, or by any information storage and retrieval system without permission in writing by the author.

NFB Publishing
119 Dorchester Road
Buffalo, New York 14213
For more information visit Nfbpublishing.com

Also by Sinéad Tyrone

NOVELS:

Walking Through The Mist
Crossing The Lough Between
Playing Each Other Home

The Space Between Notes

POETRY:

Fragility
A Song Of Ireland

For Beth, my book cover artist, my fellow adventurer, my friend. We have shared so many laughs, tears, adventures and dreams, and so much more to come. Thank you for being the inspiration for this book, for waiting patiently for it to come alive, and for being such a truly wonderful friend.

Preface

Nathaniel McCarey stood outside the stone cottage at the edge of the flax field he had just finished harvesting the week before. He'd almost lost count of how many years he had tended and harvested flax there. Was it fifteen? Seventeen? Twenty? Yes, that seemed right. Twenty long years of gazing happily over wide stretches of blue blossoms in May, worrying over them through the wind and rainstorms June and July always brought, then harvesting, de-seeding, breaking the outer stocks, cleaning, and turning the flax stalks over to Mary, his wife, for spinning and weaving, washing and laying linen cloth out on green fields for the sun to bleach. The work could be back breaking at times, and tiring. Still, when linen merchants examined the woven linens Mary had produced from flax he had grown Nathaniel felt a deep, almost overwhelming sense of pride.

He remembered when, at Lord Marris's direction, he had built the cottage out of stone dug out of the land when he first started working for the lord and landowner. He'd tried explaining his ancestors had lived on that plot of land as far back as he could remember, recited for Marris his family's bloodline and where they'd all been from. Nathaniel had made no impression on the lord, however; he'd been given a week to build the cottage and thereafter pay rent to dwell in it, with the promise that someday, if he saved enough, he could buy the cottage outright and live rent free.

Saving money over the years had been almost as hard as growing and harvesting flax. The famine years had wiped out his savings, had almost cost him his life as food had grown so scarce. Indeed, two of his children had perished and he, unable to save them, could only stand by helplessly as fever overtook them in their weakened state. After those black years, he had been more determined than ever to put aside whatever money he could, at first to provide food for his family should another crop failure ever threaten their existence. As that danger faded and his nest egg grew, he dared to dream of owning the cottage upon which he and his wife had paid rent for so many years.

Now he was about to enter town and buy the stone structure he had built, where for years he had hung his coat and laid his shoes.

Nathaniel changed from his work clothes to the one good suit he owned, the one his wife, Mary, had sewn for him evenings, after her day of spinning cloth was through. He brushed the sleeves of his buttoned-up shirt, relishing for a moment the luxurious feel of the fine, close weave, so much smoother than the coarse grain of his work shirt, imagining for a moment the fabric had been fashioned with linen threads spun from flax he himself had grown.

Standing in front of the assessor's office in Gaffney, the nearest town, Nathaniel wiped his hands against his slacks to remove the sweat that covered them, cleared his throat, took three deep breaths, then pulled the door open and stepped inside.

Joseph Williamson, the chief clerk, lifted his eyes to see who had entered. Seeing Nathaniel, Williamson inhaled, held his breath a minute, and steeled himself. What did this no count itinerant Irishman want anyway? Expecting the farmer had come to beg mercy, to not be evicted for rent nonpayment, Williamson reminded himself to take a hard line, to not be swayed by any amount of pleading or tears. Lord Marris had, after all, hired him to protect his investments in the lands he owned. Worthless farmers who drank their wages away instead of setting enough aside for their monthly obligations would not be carried forever.

"Yes? Can I help you?" Williamson waved his hand to signal Nathaniel to step closer.

"I'm here to purchase the cottage I've been renting." Nathaniel forced himself to speak clear and slow, to calm the nerves racing through him.

Stunned, Williamson did not know at first how to react. Purchase the cottage? While it's true a handful of Irishmen had found resources to purchase their residences, he'd opposed every one. He would not make an exception now.

"What's the address?" Williamson looked the records up, turning pages loudly even after he'd located the correct ledger, stalling for time. At length, he turned his attention back to Nathaniel.

"I'm sorry. Our records show a new owner has already purchased that property, both cottage and land. You should be receiving official notice in the next few days."

Too shocked to react, Nathaniel remained frozen in place.

"Was there something else?" Williamson demanded.

"I … I … I'd like to see the sale records now." Nathaniel wasn't sure he was allowed to make such a request, but he couldn't give up without a protest.

Slamming his ledger shut, Williamson snarled, "Official records are not open for review. You'll receive notice soon enough." With that he stepped away from his desk, retreating to a back room until he heard Nathaniel turn, walk away, and close the door behind him.

Walking home, Nathaniel's rage grew. He was sure he'd been lied to, that no one else had bought his place, that he had been denied because he was Irish, or because he followed the Catholic faith. He'd known friends who had been similarly denied, had thought each time they had to be wrong, there was some other explanation. Now, though, he suspected the truth, that the rumored prejudices were in fact influencing the clerk's denials.

He was so caught up in his anger he didn't hear the footsteps multiplying behind him. Along a stretch of road outside Gaffney, where it curved away from Lough Neagh and was shielded from view by a stand of oak trees, he was knocked to the ground and pummeled by more fists than he could count. Someone held his face in the dirt while another searched through his coat and pants pockets.

"Here it is!" One of his attackers called out, grabbing hold of the money Nathaniel had carried.

A different voice ordered, "Let him go, but give him something to remember us by!"

A kick to the head robbed Nathaniel of any consciousness.

Dusk had replaced daylight by the time Nathaniel's mind cleared. Rising from the ground slowly, he tested his legs, found them wobbly but strong enough to carry his weight, rubbed his arms where bruises already ached, felt a slight trace of blood along his temple where he'd been kicked and another stream of blood from a split lip. His pockets were empty. His pride deflated, he inched his way home.

"They took it all, Mary," he confirmed as she washed his bruises with a warm, wet cloth. "We've got nothing."

"We've got each other," she countered, "and our sons. We've made it through rough times before. We can start again."

Nathaniel listened to her words, and those of his brother, Patrick, who had rushed over as soon as he'd heard of the attack; he allowed them to express their anger, their frustration, all the thoughts and feelings that ran through them as they tried to come to terms with what had happened. All while they spoke, an idea sparked within him. Like a flame given air and fuel to burn, the idea took hold and blazed stronger, until at last he broke his silence and announced, "We're leaving this place! I've had enough!"

They all spoke at once then, a cacophony of questions and protests as Mary, who wanted to stay, pointed out they had no money to travel, while Patrick suggested ships to America couldn't be too costly, plenty of people had emigrated to the land whose streets were paved with gold. Bernard, Nathaniel's second oldest son, agreed with his uncle, America would give them the fresh start they needed, while Hugh, his oldest son, desired to stay, he had fallen in love and did not want to leave his Catherine behind.

"I'll take over your fields here and the rent," Hugh promised, "just in case America doesn't work out."

"Even if we're destitute there, I'll not be coming back!" Nathaniel vowed. "I've had enough! Sure, the worst jobs in America would be better than the constant mistreatment here."

Two months passed, days and weeks dragging on as Nathaniel helped neighbors with their harvest for a small share of their profits, and Mary set aside every bit she could, spending the bare minimum on marketing, making do with whatever scraps of food she could manage. Heads down and mouths closed, they both held their tongue about what had transpired, even when friends asked about the bruises Nathaniel sported days after the beating, even when Williamson, whenever he spotted them in town, sneered as if he had more than common knowledge about the attack. Even when the rumored letter of another owner of his cottage never materialized. Sixty-four days they held their peace and increased their savings. When they booked passage for three to America, Nathaniel thought to himself, "At last, I can put all the despair and fear behind me! Sure, in America I'll be able to own my own land and build a much better life."

For all his excitement, though, on the day Nathaniel, Mary and Bernard left for Belfast and the ship that would carry them across the Atlantic, Nathaniel felt a weight of sadness permeate his heart as he stood outside the stone cottage where he and Mary had raised their family. Of the four children they'd borne, only Hugh and Bernard remained, two were buried not far off, and he would now be leaving one, his oldest, behind.

"Look after things well here," he advised Hugh, laying a firm hand on his eldest son's shoulder. "Don't wait too long to make Catherine your bride. Fill this cottage with the laughter of children. Look after the fields, they'll give you what you need to get by. And mind yourself, stay away from trouble. If you change your mind at all, come join us."

HUGH McCarey continued growing flax as his father had done, but over time turned to wheat and barley crops as well. He and Catherine married, raised sons Nathaniel, James and Bernard, and a daughter, Mary Cate. When not working in the field, Hugh maintained repairs at the cottage he had taken over from his father, plastering spaces between the stones to keep the cottage warm in winter, rethatching the roof when it appeared weak, keeping the windows and door secure. While his father vowed to never return, Bernard provided updates through frequent letters, letting Hugh know his father and brother had fared well enough through farming to have a house over their heads. Bernard married and raised sons and daughters.

When Nathaniel grew old and felt his time to pass over was near, he begged Bernard to take him back to Ireland. "Just once more, I'd like to set my eyes on the land where I was born, and to see my son. I should have granted Mary that wish before she passed. Two years now it is since she's gone, and I've never forgiven myself for denying her that. Sure, Hugh would never forgive me if both of us passed without seeing him one last time."

Bernard dutifully carried out his father's wish and traveled with him back to Ireland. Four days Nathaniel spent playing with his grandchildren, dining with family, enjoying tea or a pint or two with old friends, reliving stories with Patrick, Hugh and Bernard, reveling in the hundreds of memories that sprang up like so many new plants emerging each spring from roots that had long ago taken hold.

The fourth night, before retiring, Nathaniel took Hugh aside, drawing him out to the back of the cottage where moon and stars looked down on the fields both had labored over. He felt Mary close beside him, pictured her working the flax fields with him, spinning and weaving the flax they had grown into fine linens, pictured her caring for children and cooking meals over a hearth fire, always with a smile in her eyes and a head full of wisdom to guide them. He regretted all over again that he'd never brought Mary back to see Hugh and her grandchildren.

"I never should have left," he confessed. "Your mam, she never wanted to go, only did so to appease me. My temper was hot, and I refused to bend. I should have returned sooner so your mam could see you one last time. For that I am sorry.

"You've built a fine life here for yourself, my boy. You've a lovely wife and doting children. You'll never be alone in old age. The good Lord himself has smiled upon you and blessed you."

Nathaniel ran a hand over the stone sides of the cottage behind them, allowing a wistful sigh to escape. "I remember the first day your mother and

I moved in here. We worked hard, so we did, to earn the money to buy this place. She's a fine cottage, solid and strong, and with the care you've shown she holds the warmth inside her on a stormy day. I'm that proud that you did what I could not and purchased her outright. Hold on tight to her. Land to tend to and a good solid home are all an Irishman needs to feel secure in this world. Keep this land and this cottage in the family as long as you're able."

Nathaniel passed over in his sleep that night.

Bernard returned to America after their father's funeral. Hugh remained in Ireland, saw his country transformed through the fight for independence, remained in place when Gaffney and the northern counties continued to be held by the British while the rest of Ireland gained independence. When he passed he left the cottage to his eldest son, also named Nathaniel following the traditional practice of naming firstborn sons after the father's father, with strict instructions to keep the land as a family holding. Nathaniel married and had two sons, James and Hugh.

James perished in a field in France during the second World War. Hugh, enticed by the riches one could earn working in the construction industry in America, moved to New York State. He married, but the marriage did not last past the first three years. Returning to Northern Ireland, he moved in with his father, worked as a farmhand at a local sheep farm by day, and evenings helped his father try to grow wheat; but the harvests were never abundant enough to yield a worthwhile harvest. In time, Hugh sold the field to a company interested in planting rapeseed for the canola oil that had become a profitable business.

The cottage remained in Hugh's hands.

Chapter One

Maggie McCarey hesitated outside the door to the hospital room where her mother had spent the past two and a half weeks fighting her third battle against the cancer that had invaded her body, this time spreading through her lungs and liver and into her bones. Each day her mother had grown a bit weaker and the pain had increased a degree more. Conversation between Maggie and her mother was limited now to whatever short sentences her mother could muster in between struggles to catch her breath.

With no sisters or brothers to spell her, the full burden of her mother's care had fallen on Maggie's shoulders. Her mother, Susan, had long ago completed the paperwork spelling out her final wishes, cremation instead of burial, no heroic efforts to keep her alive beyond what was reasonable, a small funeral with only close friends invited, her ashes to be cast upon the waves of Lake Erie, a favorite destination of hers and only a few hours' drive from their central Ohio home. Susan had already informed Maggie everything Susan owned would be left to her and insurance policies were in place to cover any financial needs that might remain after Susan passed. Any loose ends had been anticipated and neatly tied up through the same businesslike approach Susan had used in dealing with every other issue in her life.

The same businesslike approach that had built a wall between Maggie and her mother. For as far back as Maggie could remember, Susan had been firm, practical, efficient, almost impersonal, holding emotion and sentiment at bay, a defense system that had carried Susan through the many upheavals life had presented, but had also held Maggie at arms' length. Over the years they had developed a respectful relationship, devoid of the closeness Maggie had so often yearned for but didn't know how to obtain. At a loss for how to bridge the gap between them, Maggie had eventually discarded any questions she had so badly wanted to ask about her father, about why their marriage had ended, about Susan's life before Maggie had come along. Susan kept no family photos of her own parents or siblings, had always brushed aside Maggie's attempts to learn any information at all about them, had focused on present and future instead of looking back.

Now, standing outside Susan's hospital room door, all those unasked questions rose in Maggie's mind again. Again, and for the last time, she would have to leave them unanswered. Her mother was too weak, too consumed with fighting for her life to manage any emotional stress those questions would cause. Maggie would set her own desires for closeness and information aside and lend whatever support and strength Susan would need.

Entering the room, Maggie caught the eye of the attendant nurse who had just finished adjusting the intravenous bag that supplied a constant drip of Susan's medicine. With an almost imperceptible shake of her head, the nurse confirmed without a word what Maggie's instincts had told her the last few days. Susan had little time left.

"Hi Mom." Maggie forced sunshine into her voice. "I brought you fresh daisies. I know they're your favorite." Collecting the vase off Susan's windowsill, she threw the fading bouquet in the trash bin in the bathroom adjoining Susan's room, filled the vase with fresh water and stood the daisies up in it, then returned the vase to the windowsill. "Don't they look cheery?"

Susan offered a half smile.

"Has the doctor been in yet today? How are you feeling? Do you need anything?"

Susan gave a slight shake of her head. She motioned with her hand for Maggie to come closer, patted the side of her bed for Maggie to sit on.

Maggie thought she had never seen her mother look so serious.

"I have something to tell you and I'm short of breath, so listen carefully." Susan paused as another wave of pain swept over her, then went on, focusing her eyes not on her daughter but on the daisies Maggie had brought. They wouldn't make her confession any easier to release, but they, instead of her daughter, were easier to face.

"I've done something very unfair to you. I need to apologize and explain."

Maggie waited, curious as to what her mother might be talking about.

"Your father and I were young when we married, too naïve and inexperienced to know how to make a marriage work. We fought so much of the time; I was miserable, and he took to drinking. One night we had a horrible argument, our worst ever. He hit me, gave me a black eye and broke my cheekbone. I wasn't ever going to risk him doing that again. I divorced him and blocked him from ever contacting you. You were two at the time."

As her mother revealed details Maggie had wondered about all her life, she felt a mix of emotions: gladness that at least some of her curiosity was now being satisfied, hurt that her father had not tried over the years to reach out to her despite whatever promise he'd made to her mother so many years earlier, and sadness as she realized this confession meant her mother knew she truly was slipping away.

Then came the bombshell part of her mother's admission.

"Your father returned to his family home in Northern Ireland after our divorce. Several months ago, I received a letter informing me your father had passed and had left some property there to you. I should have told you right away, but I was dealing with chemotherapy and radiation by then, set the letter aside and then forgot about it." Susan stopped, shook her head, and resumed, "No, that's not right. The truth is I kept the letter away from you. I was afraid if you found out your father had left you property you would want to run away to Ireland and I would lose you. You and I haven't always been the closest of mothers and daughters. I know it was wrong of me and I'm sorry. I hope you'll forgive me. You'll find the letter and your father's solicitor's contact information in the middle drawer of my desk."

Exhausted from her long speech and relieved of the matter that had been pressing most on her mind, Susan rested her head against her pillow, closed her eyes, and was soon asleep.

Maggie's first instinct was to rush over to her mother's apartment and find the letter. She held off; her mother looked even more pale than she had the past several days and her breathing carried a ragged sound. The few times she woke over the two days that followed she was barely lucid, spoke in fragments Maggie was unable to make sense of, and refused all food or drink.

By the third day, Susan was gone.

As much as Maggie's relationship with her mother had been strained, Susan's passing carried with it a finality Maggie hadn't anticipated. There would be no more opportunities to clear the air between them, no way to break down barriers and resolve any outstanding issues. What was done was done forever; what had been left undone could not be tackled now.

"I didn't expect it to hit me this hard," Maggie confessed to Brianna "Bree" Halloran the next day, over the lattes and cranberry muffins Bree had brought to console her best friend. "I mean, I knew her time was limited, I knew there would be a number of things that would never be resolved and I thought I had made my peace with that, but it's much harder than I thought it would be. I feel guilty that I didn't make more of an attempt to develop a closer relationship with her."

"She didn't make it easy. Your mother was very good at running a household and managing an executive secretary position, but she expected everyone else to fall in line with what she thought their lives should be. You didn't play the game the way she thought you should. You chose teaching over secretarial or business work. You dated, but you never let any of the men you dated run your life, and when she questioned you about why your relationships didn't work out you held your ground. It would have been hard for anyone to find the cracks in her hard exterior and develop any real closeness with her."

"Maybe." Maggie took a long drink of her coffee while she thought over

Bree's words. "Still, I'll always wonder if I could have tried harder. She was more open at the end. Did I tell you she told me about my father?"

Bree almost dropped the muffin in her hands. "No! Really? What did she say?"

"They were young, they struggled, he hit her, she sent him packing." The bottom line was all Bree needed to know. Then Maggie held up the envelope she had retrieved from her mother's desk. "He passed away several months ago. His attorney sent this letter to my mother; apparently, he left me some property. I've been afraid to open this."

"Do it!" Bree had to hold herself back from grabbing the envelope and opening it for Maggie. "You won't rest until you find out what it says."

The envelope trembled in Maggie's hands as she tried to settle the nerves doing battle inside her. For forty years she'd heard nothing from or about her father. Now, in the space of three days, she knew his name, a general reference to where he lived, and that he was lost to her now. Except he wasn't completely lost. In her hands she held whatever final communication he'd wanted her to have. Her mind swirled with myriad thoughts, while inside her fear and excitement battled for control.

Maggie slid a finger under the sealed flap and withdrew the contents of the envelope bearing a Northern Ireland solicitor's name and address.

Two pieces of paper faced her.

The first was a general letter from Sean McCabe, solicitor, indicating what little she already knew: Hugh McCarey, in his final days, had drawn up a will in which he left her a small plot of land, upon which a small cottage stood, just outside the town of Gaffney, Northern Ireland. She needed to claim the property by the end of May, or it would revert to a cousin of his.

The end of May? Maggie glanced at the calendar on her mobile phone, although she already knew it was the middle of March. That didn't leave her much time!

The second piece of paper was a handwritten letter. Maggie read it through twice, then read it out loud to Bree:

Dear Maggie,

I know you have not heard from me since you were a wee child. I promised your mother I would not try to contact you; but now I am breaking that promise. I am in poor health and fear I may not have time to come visit you in person; but I want you to know I have never stopped wondering about you, have never stopped wishing someday we would connect. You are my only child. I am that sorry I treated your mother so badly when we were young and lost the opportunity to watch you grow into the lovely lass I am sure you have become.

I don't have much to leave you except my cottage and the land upon which it stands. This cottage has been in our family for generations. I trust you will find the right thing to do with it.

Please forgive me for being that poor of a father that I have neglected you all these years, no matter what promises I made to your mother when I was young.

Your father, Hugh McCarey

Maggie had little time to think of the letter or the cottage as she planned her mother's funeral, contacted her mother's closest friends, and went through the formalities that filled one's days when a loved one had passed. After the funeral, on a sunny March day she and Bree, and Susan's best friend Audrey, drove to a deserted curved beach along Lake Erie, recited a few short quotes, whispered a prayer, and cast Susan's ashes upon the waves which the lake's waters soon drank in and carried away. Maggie placed a rock upon which she had painted a daisy under a row of wild rose shrubs to the right of the beach, hoping it would remain there undiscovered for a while.

That night Maggie consumed a bottle of wine by herself, then fell asleep on the sofa, the first good night's sleep she'd had in weeks.

THE next day Maggie met with Arthur Hanley, her mother's attorney.

"I'm not sure what papers you need from me to handle my mother's estate, but I know we have to start somewhere."

"Yes. I was so sorry to hear of Susan's passing." Arthur retrieved a folder from the stack on his desk corner, opened it and pulled the top sheet of paper out. "We will need a certified copy of the death certificate when you have it. After that I'll work with you on the various forms to be signed and the process for finalizing your mother's estate.

"Your mother's will is pretty straightforward. Susan had a retirement account, and a savings account she kept in reserve. She also had a life insurance policy listing you as beneficiary. I estimate, after expenses have all been paid, you can expect to receive something in the neighborhood of two hundred thousand dollars."

Maggie stared at Arthur as if he had spoken to her in Swahili. "That can't be right. My mother never had money to spare. She was always cutting coupons, looking for bargains, stretching her dollars as far as she could; at the end of each month, she was down to her last few dollars."

"She did her best to live within her salary and not dip into her reserves. She told me once it was important to her to leave something behind for you."

"I would rather have had her leave me with happy memories instead of money." Judging by the lack of reaction on Arthur Hanley's face, Maggie knew she'd only thought the words, and much to her relief had not spoken them out loud. She told Arthur, "I never dreamed she'd leave me anything, let alone that much."

"You should wait for all of Susan's medical and other bills to be settled before you start spending your inheritance, and we should discuss tax consequences so you're prepared for that, but I can release some of the money for you in a few weeks, after we've filed her death certificate and other papers with the bank."

"Thank you." Maggie then drew out of her handbag the letter from Sean McCabe. "This was in my mother's desk. She told me about it just before she passed. Would you mind taking a look at it?"

Arthur read the letter over twice, then looked at Maggie, stunned. "Susan never mentioned your father. Did you know anything about him?"

"Not until now. I'm as surprised as you are."

"Do you mind if I make a copy of this? I can call Mr. McCabe to check on the status of the property, confirm the legitimacy of the will, explain your mother's illness and the delay in your responding to his letter before now."

"I'd appreciate it if you could call him. Thank you."

Mind swirling as she reached her car, Maggie sat behind the steering wheel several minutes trying to make sense of all the changes the last couple of weeks had brought about. She'd lost her mother, gained information she'd always wanted to know about her father although he, too, had passed, inherited a piece of property she knew nothing about somewhere in Northern Ireland, and was about to come into an unexpected windfall.

What next?

Maggie inserted her key into her car's ignition, rotated her hand forward to start the engine, then stopped herself.

Her hand was trembling, her arms felt weak, and the sidewalk edging the parking lot in front of her blurred. She felt dizzy, and wondered for a minute if she might pass out. Her stomach rumbling told her she might need food, but she knew the cause for her physical reactions ran deeper.

Maggie's whole world had been shaken. Everything she knew and trusted about her mother now felt suspect, she didn't even know the woman who had concealed an inheritance from her, who had withheld financial truths Maggie could have benefitted from knowing as she'd worried over the past several weeks if she would be able to cover all of her mother's hospital and medical expenses. The woman who might even have known where Maggie's father resided but kept that knowledge hidden, denying Maggie a chance to at the very least have a conversation with her father before he passed away. Who hid truth from Maggie out of a fear that Maggie would relocate and leave her mother alone.

Who was this woman? Maggie wished with everything in her she could march into her mother's apartment, or hospital room, and demand explanations. It was too late for that, for any kind of meaningful conversations with the woman she had known all her life, the woman she now realized she barely knew.

Her mind filled with so many new facts and thoughts, Maggie was certain of only one thing. It was Friday. There was no way she would be prepared to teach her high school English classes come Monday. As her phone rang into Daniel Harris's office, she formulated in her mind how she would ask her principal for more time off.

"Mr. Harris, I'd like to request another week off. I still have a lot to handle with my mother's passing, and to be honest it has hit me harder than I thought. The following week is spring break, I'm sure I'll be fine to return to work after that."

Daniel didn't answer right away. Maggie, sure he was about to deny her request, scrambled to think of a stronger argument to sway him. When he spoke at last, Daniel's voice sounded strained, as if immense pressure or unwanted news, or both, preyed on him.

"Maggie, as you know our district recently settled a sizable lawsuit. Because of that, each school in the district has had its budget cut for the rest of the year, effective immediately."

Maggie nodded, aware of the settlement, curious as to how that impacted her.

"This drastic cut has necessitated slashing a number of teacher positions across the board. Maggie, after spring break you won't be returning here as an English teacher. You'll receive severance pay, and the district will be in touch with you about your benefits."

Maggie felt the world spin around her. She clutched her steering wheel to keep herself grounded, to keep from completely passing out.

"No job?" She demanded of Principal Harris. "I'm let go?"

Hating this part of his job, wishing with everything in him he'd retired two years earlier when an incentive package had been offered, Daniel was well aware how hollow his next words sounded. "Maggie, you're an excellent teacher. We'll provide referrals; I'm sure you won't have a problem finding a job in another school system."

"Daniel, you know school districts around us have already filled their teaching positions for the year. Any teachers our district lays off will all be scrambling for whatever openings exist in our area. My chances of finding a job nearby are almost nonexistent." With nothing more to argue, Maggie told him, "I'll be in this weekend to clean out my desk and gather my belongings."

Chapter Two

Bree was in the midst of preparing the lasagna she had planned for dinner that evening when Maggie's call came through.

"Are you busy tonight? Do you mind if I come over?"

Best friends since grade school, Bree knew all the tones of Maggie's voice, when Maggie was happy or sad, angry or ebullient. Now, Maggie sounded devastated, as if her entire world had collapsed around her. Even when Susan was in her last days, Maggie had not sounded so desperate.

"Come over any time," Bree had responded. "You can have dinner with me."

Wondering what new crisis had so upset her friend, Bree had wine poured into two glasses, ready and waiting when Maggie pulled into her driveway.

"I just lost my job." Maggie waved away the wine glass Bree held out. "I can't believe it. Just like that I'm out of a job!"

Bree was so stunned she didn't know what to say at first. She hadn't expected this. "What happened?"

Sinking down into the chair where she'd tossed her coat and handbag, Maggie's eyes filled with tears. "You know the lawsuit the school district just lost? Well, the result is that each school has to cut positions effective immediately. Mine was one of the positions they decided could be let go."

"That doesn't seem fair! Couldn't they at least wait until the end of the school year? What about your classes, what happens to them?"

Maggie took a long drink of wine while trying to sort out an answer. "The district doesn't have the money up front to pay the settlement. They can't put off the first installment until September, they need to start now. I guess they'll split my classes up among the other teachers. I didn't ask."

The tears Maggie had been fighting back ever since speaking with Daniel Harris spilled over, leaking out of the corners of her eyes, tracing thin tracks down her cheeks. Wiping them away with the back of her hand, she confessed to Bree, "I don't know what I'm going to do! There aren't enough teaching jobs in our area as it is; with more teachers beside me being let go, the competition for jobs will be fierce. I might have to move away."

"Or change professions." Bree ignored the "have you lost your mind" look Maggie shot her, and continued, "You're smart, you have knowledge and experience behind you. You've got self-confidence galore. You just need to figure out what your next dream is and go for it!"

"The only dream I had was teaching."

"I disagree. You've also mentioned opening a coffee shop, or a bookstore. Or working as a travel agent."

"Or becoming an artist or a singer. Or an international photographer." Maggie would have laughed if her situation wasn't so dire. "Those were all pipe dreams, castles in the air. They aren't practical ideas."

"Maybe not practical," Bree agreed, "but the point is, you have a lot of know how, more than you realize right now. You can do anything you set your mind to."

As lasagna baked in the oven, as they tossed lettuce, tomato, cucumber, croutons and slivered almonds in a huge salad bowl, Bree let Maggie vent over her job loss and fear of what to do next. When they sat down to eat, Bree changed the narrative.

"Do you remember how devastated I was when Carter left me?"

"Of course! That was such a horrible time for you."

Horrible was a huge understatement, Bree thought as unwanted memories flooded her mind. Rumors whispered behind her back but loud enough for her to hear as she shopped for groceries or ordered coffee at the café in town. Carter's longer and longer hours "at work," which turned out to be lies upon lies. Carter requesting a meeting with her in the middle of the day while their then-teenage twins Regan and Riley were at school, announcing that his secretary, Lyla, was pregnant, he was the father, and he was filing for divorce from Bree so he could marry Lyla.

"Do you remember what you told me the night he broke the news to me?"

Maggie wasn't sure. She'd offered so many words of advice to Bree over the last few years she couldn't remember which Bree referred to now.

"No, what did I tell you?"

"You said there are times our lives will fall apart in a million pieces and we won't have a clue how to glue those pieces back together. You said at those times we have to dig deep, very deep inside us and find the strength and ability to rebuild our lives." Bree paused to give Maggie time to digest those words, then continued. "I don't know that I've dug deep enough yet, I feel like I'm still floundering a bit, I haven't fully put my life back together; but I've climbed far enough out of the black hole I was in after my divorce that I can start to see daylight. I can start to look at possibilities for my future."

Maggie considered Bree's advice. Had her life fallen in a deep hole yet? She wasn't sure; but it sure had undergone monumental upheaval. "I just feel like all the solid ground underneath me is shifting, like a constant landslide. Before I found out about my job, I met with my mother's attorney. You know how she always made it seem like she was low on money? She wasn't. She's leaving me a pretty sizeable inheritance."

Bree almost choked on her wine. "Are you kidding?"

Maggie shook her head. "Bree, I was so surprised. I found out she had a retirement account and insurance policy, the proceeds of which will come to me. Here I've been worrying about how to pay my mother's expenses, and not only will they be paid, but I'll have plenty of money left over!"

"That doesn't sound like a bad problem to have."

"I just wish my mother had told me about these things. I shouldn't have had to hear about it from her attorney, or to find out on her deathbed that my father left me something. Why would she do that, Bree? Why wouldn't she just come out and tell me these things?"

Bree set her fork down. "Maggie, your mother has always been a puzzle, hasn't she? She always was secretive, always wanted to handle things her way."

For a full minute, Maggie studied the pearl ring on her right hand, the one her mother had given her for her birthday twenty years earlier. She thought back on so many good times she'd had with her mother, as well as the tense times, the times it was hard to push past the wall her mother sometimes raised when a conversation took a turn she didn't like. "I know she wasn't easy," Maggie admitted now, "but I thought I understood her, thought I knew almost everything about her. Now I feel like I didn't know her at all."

Bree knew what her best friend meant. So many times, Bree herself had thought she knew people, only to end up at a loss when they acted contrary to what she expected. Carter, of course, turned her world upside down with his affair and subsequent divorce. Then there were her twins, Regan and Riley. When they were young, she knew all their moves and moods, knew just how to read them. As teenagers, their moods were often decipherable, although at times their decisions and actions surprised her. Now, in their second year at universities, they seemed more full of surprises than ever. Bree sometimes attributed this to the distance between them, with Riley in veterinary school in Tennessee, and Regan studying accounting in Chicago. Just this week, they had each done what she would never have anticipated.

"What would you think if I changed my major?" Regan had asked her when he called Tuesday night.

Bree knew enough to hear him out before giving her opinion. "What would you change it to?"

"Forestry." There was no denying the excitement in his voice. "I really want to get a job in one of the national parks!"

Bree had visions of the financial security she wished for Regan flying out the window. "Have you thought long and hard on this? There are plenty of jobs for accountants, but how many jobs could you find in the forestry field?"

"I've been researching this since last fall. There are a good number of jobs in forestry, plenty to go around for the number of people entering the field. I might not get a national park right away; I'd have to work up to that."

Regan's confession that he'd been thinking of this for months jarred Bree. "Why didn't you ask me about this when you were home for Christmas?" After a long pause, Regan admitted, "I was afraid you'd be upset with me."

Bree had felt a wave of shame then, wondering what about her would ever make her son afraid to tell her anything. Hadn't she always encouraged his and his sister's goals, even the ones that made little or no sense, like when he'd wanted to be a professional skateboarder, or Riley had wanted to be an opera singer.

To show her son she supported him now, Bree had asked, "Do they offer courses in that field where you are now?"

"No. I would have to transfer to another university. I want to go to Denver."

Colorado seemed to be the other side of the world from her home in Ohio. Panic rose inside Bree as she thought of her son moving so far away. If he did succeed in receiving a degree in forestry, she was sure she'd never talk him into moving back home. Another part of the world she had built around her fell away, replaced by a layer of fear.

Wednesday, Riley had called with her own news.

"You don't mind if I don't come home for spring break, do you?"

Mind? Of course Bree minded! She'd looked forward to seeing her daughter after the long months since Riley had been home for Christmas. She had planned shopping with Riley, a theater outing, and plenty of late-night movie and girl talk sessions. Surely Riley knew how much Bree depended on that.

Still, she found it hard to deny her daughter.

"Did you have other plans?" It was a stupid, redundant question, but the best Bree could manage at the moment.

"Peter wants to take me to Virginia Beach, to the ocean. Oh, please say yes, Mom! You haven't met Peter yet, but you'd like him. He's sweet, and super handsome, and I really want to go. Please say yes!"

"Who is Peter? You've never mentioned him before?"

"Just a friend," Riley had said at first, then admitted, "okay, he's my boyfriend."

"How long has he been your boyfriend?" Bree wanted to know, thinking if her daughter had only met him a few weeks ago there was no way Bree would agree to the Virginia Beach excursion.

"We've been dating since December."

Being run over by an eighteen-wheeler would not have hurt Bree worse than the revelation that her daughter, in all the conversations they'd shared over the past three months, had never once mentioned a boy she was clearly serious about. Why had her daughter felt the need to hide him from her?

"What is it about Peter you're afraid I won't like?" Bree demanded. "You obviously think there's something about him I'm not going to approve of, or you would have mentioned him before."

"It's not like that, Mom! It's just, well, I wasn't sure how serious he was about me so I haven't said anything to a lot of people, just wanted to see how things would work out." Bree might have been appeased with that if Riley hadn't added, "There are a lot of things about my life I don't tell you."

It took Bree several deep breaths to recover from that statement. "What else don't I know?"

Riley had backpedaled then, telling her mother, "Nothing important, forget I said that."

Warnings of all sorts flashed through Bree's mind. "Riley, be careful. I don't care how long you've known this boy, this is a crazy world, full of risks and dangerous situations. People aren't always what they seem."

Impatient with warnings she'd heard a dozen times before, and infused with her father's stubbornness and independence, Riley pushed back. "I know, Mom. You've told me how many times? Peter's not like that. He's a good person. And," Riley pulled out her ace card, "I don't really need your permission, I could go no matter what you say."

Bree had no choice but to agree. "Please promise you'll keep in touch with me and let me know where you'll be staying in case …". In case what? There was no use spelling out the various horrific events that could occur. Riley would only dig her heels in more and refuse to provide places and contact information. "Just in case I need to call for anything," Bree finished.

"I will, Mom." Riley had promised. "Don't worry. And thanks!"

Recalling those two conversations, Bree admitted to Maggie now, "I don't know that we ever really know people as much as we think we do. Maybe there are sides to people they always hold back, some part of themselves they tuck away and don't reveal unless they're forced to. Maybe it's self preservation, or something like that. Oh, you and I aren't like that, we tell each other everything. There are no hidden corners between us. But others, I don't know, maybe they're afraid of being rejected, or afraid of admitting parts of themselves or their lives others might not approve of.

"I can't answer for your mother. She should have told you certain things. She was a pretty complex person. Maybe she was afraid if you really knew her you wouldn't like her. You were all she had; fear of losing you would have been a large risk hanging over her. Not that it would make her right to hide things from you, but maybe it would make it all a little more understandable."

Maggie absorbed Bree's words while she finished the lasagna Bree had baked. Bree told Maggie about Regan's decision to transfer to Colorado and Riley's spring break trip to Virginia Beach, and that she'd learned Carter's new wife was pregnant again. Maggie told Bree about her plan to clear out her desk at school over the weekend, and how she hoped in the coming week to start cleaning through the papers, refrigerator and food pantry at her mother's apartment.

Bree waited until they had settled back into the living room with toffee cheesecake and hazelnut coffee before returning to the topic of what kind of jobs Maggie could do next.

"You could become a tutor, Maggie. Or an editor, or even a blogger or writer, or a business writing consultant. You could work at a bookstore in the city, that's only a half hour away."

"Those are all good ideas," Maggie agreed. "I don't know, I'm too all over the place emotionally to make a decision right now."

"Of course you are. You've been through plenty the past few weeks. These are just ideas; take your time before choosing what to do next."

An idea struck Bree then, which she shared with her friend. "You have plenty of free time right now, and money available. You should go to Ireland and check out this property you've inherited."

Maggie took a long sip of her coffee while turning the idea over in her mind. "I could do that, couldn't I?"

"Not only could, you absolutely should!" Then Bree teased, while hoping Maggie would take her up on the idea, "You should have someone with you. You have no idea what you'd be facing. Regan and Riley are both spending their spring breaks elsewhere; I could go with you!"

In all the turmoil of the past few days, Maggie hadn't given thought to traveling to Ireland to view the property she'd been left. Now, Bree's idea lit the first bright light Maggie had felt for several weeks. This would be the perfect time to go, she realized, before another job tied her schedule up, before the hundreds of commitments and demands life usually carries ate up her time. Before it was too late, and the property passed to someone else. She was worn out, physically, mentally and emotionally. A break would be nice. Plus, it would be fun to travel with Bree, instead of going alone.

"I like that idea!" Maggie agreed. "Think we could plan a trip that fast? We're talking about leaving in just a few days!"

Bree almost tripped over the coffee table as she jumped up with excitement. "Are you kidding? We can have this booked before you know it!"

Chapter Three

Patrick McCarey stood before the low, one-story cottage on the outskirts of Gaffney, a small town near Lough Neagh, Northern Ireland's largest freshwater lough. He thought the cottage could use a fresh coat of whitewash, the wooden front door should be re-stained and varnished, the windows should be cleaned and their wood frames repainted. Inside, he knew several repairs would have to be undertaken before he could turn the cottage into a bed and breakfast. All that would be handled when the cottage was his.

If the cottage was his.

He knew the history of the cottage by heart, how it had been built by his great-grandfather Nathaniel, then passed on from oldest son to oldest son. The direct line of possession went through his cousin, Hugh; his own father, Bernard, had accepted that fact and purchased his own home when Patrick was a child.

Over the years, Patrick had little thought of possessing the place. When his cousin Hugh passed away, he expected the place would be handed down to Hugh's daughter in America. However, almost a year later, the girl had yet to take possession of her inheritance. If the cottage wasn't claimed in a couple more months, it would pass to him.

Oh, the plans he had for that place! After running through the list of renovations it needed, he would give the interior a fresh coat of paint, update its furnishings, then register it as a bed and breakfast for travelers who visited Ireland and Northern Ireland every year.

As he stood before the cottage now, he allowed his hopes to rise. So much in his life had not turned out as he hoped; his son, James, was living somewhere in Portugal now and only contacted Patrick when he was in need of money; his ex-wife, Peg, had landed on her feet after their divorce three years earlier and was now working as a secretary for a large business in Lurgan; while he himself had lost his job in construction and only managed occasional part time employment as a delivery person for local retailers.

Oh, the fault was his, he knew. Too many years given to drinking his pay away, too many fights with Peg, too many past due bills and too little time giving Peg the attention and affection she craved; it was no wonder she'd divorced him and moved on to a happier life. Only the shock of losing her woke him up to the need to turn his life around. He'd been away from the drink nearly two years now. For all the hard work of giving up alcohol, though, he had little to show for it. He was still just scraping by.

The bed and breakfast idea was his only chance of building a better life. He could not buy property on his own; he didn't have the money for it. He could, however, manage if Hugh's cottage went to him.

The call he'd received from Sean McCabe, Hugh's solicitor, had to be a good sign that the American lass had at last been in touch and wanted no part of property in a country far away from her own home. For a minute longer Patrick stood in front of the cottage, visualizing how he would turn it into a successful business. Then he turned his feet towards Gaffney and McCabe's office.

SEAN McCabe sat behind his oak desk replaying in his mind for the seventh time the phone call that had come in earlier that morning. While the call was a relief to him and would mean less work on his part, Patrick McCarey would have a much different reaction. The only thing for it was to call Patrick in, inform him, and pray he didn't go into a rage.

He rehearsed in his mind a half dozen ways to tell Patrick. In the end, once Patrick was seated across from him, Sean just said, "I've heard from Hugh's daughter's attorney in America. She'll be here in a day or two to claim her inheritance."

Puzzled, Patrick responded, "A week ago you said you were sure the cottage would be mine."

"I said I hadn't heard from Hugh's daughter, time was running out and there was a fair chance it would come your way."

Patrick could feel the anger rise in him and fought to control it. "I've made plans around what you said! I was counting on that cottage to give me a fresh start! What am I supposed to do now?"

"You'll stay out of her way, let her view the cottage and make up her mind. She lives in America, Patrick. She has a job and a life there; my guess is she'd be hard pressed to give that up and move thousands of miles to a country she doesn't know anything about."

Patrick turned Sean's words over in his mind and saw a glimmer of hope. "Are you saying there's a chance she'll decide to decline the property? Is that it?"

"I'm saying leave her be, let things run their course, and you might end up with what you've wanted after all."

FLYING over the Irish countryside, Maggie looked down upon a patchwork field of green and tan with occasional spots of blue that appeared to be lakes. What looked like dots from overhead turned out to be trees and small houses as the plane lowered itself closer to the ground. Just outside the Dublin airport, Maggie was amused to find cows chewing contentedly on grass; she wondered what they thought of so many objects zooming over their heads. Did they even notice? Or had they grown so used to the noise it no longer fazed them?

"How long will you be in Ireland?" The Customs agent asked Maggie, in line ahead of Bree. When she answered, "Two or three weeks," he scrutinized her. "You don't have a return date?"

"Not yet." Afraid she'd just landed herself and Bree in trouble, she explained, "I have some business to conduct in Northern Ireland, an inheritance to straighten out. I'm not quite sure how long it will take and didn't want to commit to a flight home then find out I needed more time."

"What's the nature of your inheritance?"

Maggie handed to the agent the cover letter Arthur Hanley had provided, outlining the property she'd come into possession of, and the name of the attorney in Northern Ireland who was handling the matter.

"Very well." The Customs officer returned the letter to her, stamped her passport, and handed that back to her as well. "Mind you don't stay in our country longer than ninety days."

Picking up their suitcases and renting the car Bree had booked for them went smoothly, and soon they were on their way outside of Dublin, with Maggie behind the wheel.

"I can't believe we're here!" Bree gazed at the views outside their windows as Maggie maneuvered their rental car off the motorway and onto a smaller highway. "Remember all those Irish movies we've watched, and all the times we wondered if Ireland could really be that beautiful? Everything here is as lovely as we saw in those movies, even more so."

"Are you sure you don't mind that we're putting business first before exploring Dublin and some of the popular tourism spots?"

"Not at all! It's better to get your property matter sorted so you can relax and enjoy whatever we do after."

"I thought so too." Maggie managed her first roadway roundabout, then asked Bree, "Tell me again about the places you've booked for us to stay at."

Bree pulled up the confirmation emails on her phone. "I found a bed and breakfast ten minutes away from Gaffney, where the property you now own is located. I've booked that for a week, it looks like a pretty place and very convenient."

"We're sharing the room, right?"

"Yes, our room has twin beds."

"That sounds like a good choice."

Bree waited while Maggie navigated their car through two roundabouts, then announced, "We both agreed we'd like to stay one night in a castle; I found one about a half hour away and booked a night at the end of our first week."

Maggie took her eyes off the road just long enough to flash a concerned look Bree's way. "Did you go over our budget for that?"

"No." Bree glanced again at the photo of Allynwood Castle which was included in the confirmation email. "It's not the most glamorous castle, but it's authentic, and since we're traveling off season it's affordable."

"Can you believe we're even staying in a castle?" Maggie's emotions ran from nervous as she drove foreign roads and on the opposite side of the road from what she was used to, to apprehensive over the prospect of what she would find had been left to her, too excited to be traveling at all after so many months of not being able to plan even a night out with friends. "I never imagined traveling to Ireland, let alone sleeping in a castle!"

Thankful for GPS directions, Maggie and Bree drove over roads lined with wild fuchsia hedges and golden gorse shrubs, past green and gold fields and farms with worn barns and houses. They passed through small villages with pubs and shops they noted to investigate later, and more sizable towns whose narrow roads and roundabouts increased Maggie's nervousness.

Too early to check into the bed and breakfast room they had reserved, Maggie and Bree chose to drive straight through to Gaffney, where the attorney who held the key to Maggie's property was located.

"I'm sorry to stop in without an appointment," she apologized when Sean McCabe entered the reception area of his office. "We weren't sure how our timing would work out, what with landing at the airport, renting our car, and then driving here."

"Not a problem." He led them into his office and pointed to chairs for them to sit on. "How did you find the drive?"

"I'm not too sure about those roundabouts!" Maggie gave a light laugh. "My friend Bree, here, was an excellent copilot."

Bree protested, "The GPS system guided us. If that goes down, my copilot skills are nonexistent."

Sean pulled Maggie's folder from the stack on the corner of his desk. "I'd almost lost hope we'd hear from you."

"I'm sorry. I didn't know about my father, or any of this, until recently."

"I sent a letter to your mother months ago. It was the only way your father knew to reach you."

Maggie still found the next words hard to say. "My mother was battling cancer the last several months. She only told me about the letter a couple of weeks ago, before she passed away."

"I am sorry." Sean allowed Maggie a moment to breathe, to settle her feelings before continuing, "The cottage is a pleasant one, about a mile outside of town. I haven't inspected it inside, it may need some repairs, some fresh paint. I've reviewed the records enough to know it has been in your family since your great-great-grandfather built it in the 1830s."

Maggie tried to imagine a connection to anything for that long a period of time. With her mother, she had moved twice to different states, and three times to different apartments while growing up. Her mother's parents had no long-standing attachments to homes; she'd only visited their Michigan home once, after which they'd moved to a smaller ranch style home which she'd never seen before they passed. Even the condominium Maggie lived in now had only been hers the past seven years. Nor was her mother one to keep many possessions that connected her to the past; the only item Maggie knew the history of was a copper teapot, creamer, sugar bowl and platter her mother once told her belonged to a great aunt.

A cottage almost two hundred years old? Maggie couldn't even fathom anything with that much history behind it.

"Can you tell me anything about my father? I don't know much about him."

Sean studied the woman seated across from him. She was tall, but not too much so, and slender, much like Hugh was. Her medium brown hair matched his, as did her blue eyes. He wondered if she carried his temperament, or whatever her mother's had been.

"Hugh was a quiet man. He served several years in the army. When he returned home, he found work with a concrete company. He kept to himself most of the time."

"Did he ever remarry?"

"No. He had the odd girlfriend or two but spent most of his time alone."

Surprised that she was relieved to learn this, Maggie returned to the matter of the cottage. "My attorney mentioned you have the key to the cottage. I don't know what I'll do with it, I can't imagine moving this far away, but I should at least look at it before I decide."

Sean handed the key to her and pointed out the window. "If you follow this main road to the right, just beyond town on your left you'll find it."

"Thank you. Is there anything else you need from me at this point?"

"No. Keep in mind the May deadline. Whether you choose to keep the cottage or not, I'll have some papers for you to sign."

LOCATED along the western side of Lough Neagh, Gaffney stood surrounded by flax fields long abandoned when Northern Ireland's linen industry collapsed, fields that had now become wetlands and wasteland. Comprised of one main street and four narrow side streets, the main thoroughfare contained a coffee and sandwich café, a corner store, a post office, and a fish and chip shop. Along one side street was a small school, another side street included a petrol station and a clothing consignment shop. Most of the buildings were light grey or tan stucco; while Gaffney lacked some of the brightly colored painted buildings of other towns she and Bree had passed through, Maggie was pleased to see many of the second story windows were dressed with colorful curtains instead of traditional lace coverings.

Maggie and Bree followed the main road out, as Sean had directed. At the edge of town, a small stand of trees rose on the left; just beyond that Hugh's cottage appeared. Easing their car into the narrow driveway alongside the right edge of the property, Maggie parked, and she and Bree stepped outside to survey what Maggie had inherited.

In front of the cottage a stone wall outlined a small garden area. "I don't know why they filled the dirt in here with gravel," Maggie mused. "It could have made a very pretty garden."

"You could do that if you keep the cottage." Bree studied the one-story structure. "The outside needs fresh paint, this white looks dull and dirty."

"I wonder why my father kept the front door brown. So many of the houses we've passed have bright, colorful doors." Maggie paused at the door, afraid to go in although she wasn't sure what there was to fear. Surprised to find her hand trembling the slightest bit as she fit the key into the lock, Maggie turned the bolt, opened the front door, and led Bree inside.

Two rooms were visible from the central room they stepped into, one on each side. Stepping first into the room to their left, they found a bedroom with a full-size bed, four drawer dresser, wooden chair and small desk. Down the narrow hallway between the bedroom and the central room, they found a second, slightly larger bedroom with similar furnishings. Where the window in the first bedroom looked out over the front of the house, the second bedroom's window looked out over a back garden.

Behind the central room another narrow hallway led to a small bathroom. "Hmmm, tub but no shower," Bree noted. "How will you wash your hair?"

"If I was going to stay here, I'd figure that out. You know I prefer showers."

To the right of the bathroom, on the other side of the central room, a kitchen ran along the full end of the house. Dark cupboards hung in contrast to the white walls; a worn gold flecked counter ran on both sides of the sink. A small refrigerator stood under the counter at one end; under the other end was a clothes washer. A white enamel stove occupied one end of the room. At the other end, the one visible by the central room, a round wooden table and four chairs waited for someone to occupy them.

Returning to the central room, Maggie and Bree took in the small iron framed fireplace set in the back wall, the aged sofa and matching chair set opposite the fireplace with a small low wooden table in front of them, and two windows framing the front doorway.

Bree, with her keen eye for interior decorating, was quick to note the cottage's flaws. "That kitchen needs the most help. You should replace the cupboards, update the sink and counter. The linoleum on the floor, I'd pull that right out and either do a hardwood laminate or an updated slate or stone tile. The light fixtures should all be replaced with something newer, more stylish."

While Bree continued listing repairs and updates Maggie should consider, Maggie's mind was drawn away. She ran a hand along the back of one of the kitchen chairs and thought how her father had sat there many times over the years. She wondered which of the tea mugs or plates inside one of the cupboards he might have used. Which of the bedrooms was his? In the central room, she pictured him spending chilly nights in front of a fire and wondered if he'd had friends over to share the evening with, or preferred a good book and quiet night.

Did he ever think of her? Did he ever wish he'd remained with her mother and watched Maggie grow up? His note indicated some remorse, but Maggie wondered now how deep that ran or was it just the regret of a man who knew his time was limited and he would soon answer for how he lived his life.

Maggie shook her head to clear her mind. All the questions she wondered over had no answers and would not help her determine her course of action now. She returned her attention to Bree. "Maybe we should make a list of all your suggestions. I can either hand the list over to a real estate agent if I decide to sell; or on the off chance I keep this place, it will help me prioritize what needs to be done first."

GRATEFUL for the bed and breakfast proprietor's suggestion, and recognizing they were exhausted after their long flight over and the drive north, Maggie and Bree had an early dinner at a restaurant around the corner from the place that would be their home for the week. As they ate, Bree noticed her friend was unusually quiet. She let it pass while they ate, but as they ended their meal with a cup of tea, she called Maggie on it.

"You're a million miles away tonight. Or are you just ready to fall asleep here and now?"

Maggie drew her attention away from the wall opposite them and back to Bree. "I'm sorry. I was just thinking about the house." After another long stretch of silence, she asked Bree, "Have you ever visited a place you never had been to before and felt an instant connection so deep inside you knew you belonged there more than anyplace else on the planet?"

"No, I can't say that I have."

"Today I stepped into my father's house. The father I'd been curious about for so long. I walked into what had been his world, and something happened to me, some kind of connection was made. I know it's hard for you to imagine, it's hard for me to even try to explain; but the feeling was real. I can't even name it, but I feel like all my life I've been looking for an anchor for my soul, a place where I really belonged. Today I felt like I found that."

Bree tried to imagine what Maggie was feeling. She couldn't. She'd been born and lived all her life in Corona, Ohio; her roots there ran deep as the juniper shrubs she'd had removed several years back, whose fibrous veins ran so far down in the soil it took a heavy chain attached to the back of a truck to pull the shrubs out. "Maybe your sensitivities are just heightened now, as you know for the first time you have an ancestral history here," she suggested, hoping what she offered helped Maggie find clarity. "Your mind may have combined ancestral links and newness of discovery more than a sense of belonging."

Maggie wasn't convinced. She chose not to debate the matter, or disagree with Bree, but to allow whatever she was experiencing inside to run its course, to either mature to a fully developed internal connection, or to fade away.

PATRICK had seen the two women park in front of the house that should have been his. He'd watched from where he'd pulled his car in several parking spots away from the house, where he could observe without being detected, as the two strangers unlocked the front door and disappeared inside.

The brown-haired one with the key, she must be his distant cousin. He had no clue who the second woman, with golden hair, was. They remained inside the cottage for almost an hour. Was that a good sign, he wondered? Had they had their fill of inspecting the property and decided they had little interest in retaining possession of it? The women appeared not as young as he'd imagined; sure, they were settled in their lives back home and would not want to be burdened with a house halfway across the world from where they lived and, after touring the house, would realize the impracticality of hanging onto it.

Unless . . . Patrick's mind ran miles ahead of him; he tried to call his wayward thoughts back and rein them in, but they would have none of his control. Unless Irish magic had worked its charms and drawn the women under its spell, inspiring them to leap into some grand adventure regarding "his" house.

With no way of reading what ran through their minds, or predicting what course of action they might be plotting, Patrick had no choice but to follow Sean's advice, to stay out of their way until their plans were revealed.

Chapter Four

Bree woke to find two voicemails, one each from Riley and Regan. She listened to each one twice, her anger rising with each replay.

"Mom! Where are you? My plans fell through; I came home for break and you're not anywhere around! Call me right away!"

Riley sounded more put off than panicked. Bree could picture her standing in the kitchen, hands on hips, face in a scowl as her mother-servant was not at her usual constant beck and call.

I told you three times I was going away, Bree thought. It's not my fault you weren't listening.

Regan's voice carried the same casual tone she'd grown accustomed to hearing. "Hey Mom, I decided to skip Colorado and come home for break. Not sure where you are now; will you be home for dinner?"

Of course not! You'd know that if you paid any more attention to what I say than your sister does! While his sister pouted, he'd be scrounging through cupboards for any snack that would tide him over until mom came home to rescue him from starvation.

Eight in the morning in Ireland meant three a.m. in Ohio. Bree knew she should wait a few hours to call home; she was too angry, though, to wait that long to respond. Texting them both, she explained once again she was in Ireland with Maggie and would be home in several days.

She almost dropped her phone when it rang thirty seconds after sending the text.

"Mom, how could you go running off and leave me and Regan alone on our break?"

Regan, chiming in as his sister's phone was set on speaker, added, "You could at least have let us know!"

"I did let you know! I left you both voicemail messages, neither one of you responded!"

"And you didn't think to call us again?"

"Riley, if you and your brother will check I left you each voicemails and texts explaining my plans."

Riley would not let go. "I think it's pretty selfish of you to go away when you knew our breaks were coming up!"

At that, Bree exploded! "Selfish? Ever since you two were born everything in my life has revolved around you! I've always been there for you! How many times have I dropped whatever I was doing to help you out? I've ignored my own needs and wants so I could make sure you both had anything and everything you ever wanted! And both of you told me you're not going to come home on break, not thinking maybe I would be missing you since I haven't seen either of you since Christmas! Me, selfish? I think you better take a look at yourselves on that score. It's the middle of the night there. You two should get some sleep. I'm going to get some breakfast with Aunt Maggie. You can call or text me later today."

With that, Bree hung up. "I'm sorry you had to hear that, Maggie."

Maggie, who had watched and listened for years how often Bree had bent over backwards for her son and daughter, replied, "I'm not! It's about time you straightened those two out a bit."

MAGGIE and Bree returned to the cottage after breakfast, knowing first glances didn't always catch all the details of a house. With a more critical eye, Maggie noticed repairs the cottage would need that she had missed the day before. Trim around the exterior of the house's windows and front door should be caulked, and a crack curving through one of the bedroom windows meant a pane needed replacement. The hardwood floors in the central room were worn beyond what simple varnishing would improve. The kitchen floor linoleum Bree had noted the day before would need more immediate replacement; spidery cracks in the ceilings of each of the rooms could use fresh plaster, and water stains in the ceilings of both bedrooms hinted at leaks in the roof.

"Whether I sell the cottage or keep it, I'll have to address the roof first," Maggie commented as she jotted items in a notebook. "Then the floors, then painting the trim and front door. I was thinking of blue for the door to make it stand out a bit more. What do you think?"

"Do you mean dark blue, navy? Or a turquoise blue?"

Maggie shook her head, her eyes looking past Bree to something she couldn't see at the moment. "Something softer, like the blue of the ocean."

Bree considered the idea and smiled. "That would look nice."

Maggie sank into the armchair in the central room. "I wonder if Sean McCabe could recommend a roofer and some other repairmen for me." Stopping mid-sentence, she turned to Bree. "I'm getting ahead of myself, aren't I? If I don't keep this place I could sell the cottage as is, and let the new owners handle whatever needs doing."

Even as she spoke, the words "sell" and "new owners" jarred something inside her, some sense that selling the cottage was the wrong step to take. She couldn't explain it, didn't even understand it herself. She only knew deep inside her that she could not sell what her father had left her.

Maggie had no sense of her father's family's lineage, what other relatives might also be linked to him. Surely there were others. Yet of all those he might have left the cottage to, he had chosen her. A daughter he had not seen in decades. She might never understand why he'd made that choice. She only knew she was here, in a place that was important to him, in a place that connected her to him, and that was not easily let go of.

Sitting in the cottage's central room, a vision came to her. A room full of books, a gathering of people, soft conversations and joy filling the space around them.

All her life, Maggie had had a deep love affair with books. She remembered her earliest visit to a library when she was five years old, how she'd felt she had walked into a vast treasure room. Everywhere she looked, books there called out to her. On one display stand was a book about birds; even now she could see the image of a robin's nest with three soft blue eggs in it. She could even recall the smell of the cellophane cover that protected that and other books.

Growing up as an only child, books had been her closest friends, aside from Bree. Books could take her anywhere in the world on exciting adventures, or tell stories that related to her deepest inner feelings, helping her understand herself, helping her know she was not alone after all.

Wherever she had traveled over the years, bookstores had been among her favorite places to visit; she always purchased at least a couple of books during her travels, and found the smallish bookstores especially appealing, soaking in as much as she could of their friendly atmospheres, warm vibes, and shelves filled with unimaginable prizes.

She had often wondered what it would be like to operate a small bookstore. Now, sitting in the cottage her father had left her, the idea struck again. She pictured herself filling this central room with bookshelves lined with books for sale, and people from Gaffney and surrounding areas stopping in to browse, have a chat, perhaps a cup of tea.

It was a pipe dream to be sure, but an appealing one.

While Maggie sat in the armchair, staring at the unlit fireplace and contemplating her best course of action, Bree's phone rang again. This time her ex-husband's name appeared on the screen.

"Yes?" She demanded, reserving politeness for others who had not hurt her so deeply. Every muscle in her body tightened, preparing for battle, an involuntary reaction she'd developed ever since the divorce.

"When are you coming home?" Carter barked back.

"I'm fine, thank you." Bree countered, knowing her correction of his lack of social graces would only make him angrier.

"Never mind that!" Carter ignored her remark. "What kind of mother are you, leaving two children home alone?"

"Excuse me?"

"I've had Riley calling up, crying because you left her alone when she came home for break, and Regan asking if he can borrow money for food. Where are you and when will you be home?"

Bree could feel the blood rise hot in her face. "Children? They're both in their twenties now! They've spent two years in college, they know how to fend for themselves. I've talked to them, they know where I am. If they need anything, maybe you should step up as their father and help them out."

"I can't believe you're being so irresponsible!" Carter spat out.

"Irresponsible?" Bree was shouting by now. "That's rich, coming from you! I didn't have an affair with my secretary, get her pregnant, then abandon my family to marry her! That's irresponsible!" Forcing herself to calm down, Bree continued, "Regan and Riley both told me they weren't coming home for break. Maggie and I made other plans. It's not my fault the kids changed their plans last minute and came home. For once in your life take some responsibility and be there for whatever they need."

With that, Bree hung up.

Maggie, who had heard Bree's end of the conversation and had a fair idea of what was going on, waited for Bree to explain or comment on whatever Carter had said when the phone call ended. Instead, Bree lowered herself onto the sofa and stared at the wall, drumming her fingers on the sofa's upholstered arm. They sat in silence for a good ten minutes or so, before Maggie broke the tension.

"Let's go take a drive somewhere and see some of the Irish scenery we've heard so much about." Maggie pulled her phone out and opened a map of the general area they were in. "Lough Neagh is close by, we could try for a boat trip on the lake; we could drive to Armagh, nearby, and check out St. Patrick's Cathedral; or we could head north a bit to the Antrim Coast, there's plenty of adventure there."

"The coast!" Bree could not get her words out quick enough. "Anything along the coast would be great! Watching the ocean might calm me down."

The map on Maggie's phone indicated three main points of interest: a rope bridge, a castle ruin, and an area called Giant's Causeway. She and Bree researched each, decided they were not brave enough for the rope bridge, and the Causeway looked fascinating but they didn't want to rush the experience. They chose Dunluce Castle as their first exploration destination.

Much the same as when they drove from Dublin to Gaffney, Maggie and Bree passed fields of varying shades of green dotted with small whitewash or stone homes, or occasional white wool sheep marked with colored dye, a few cattle here and there, fields of gold where rapeseed crops blossomed, and walls of stone or hedge separating fields. They passed through a couple of towns bigger than the one Maggie's house was set near, where a dozen cars parked along the main road was a crowd. Shifting from the solid cover of light grey that had started the day, to patches of grey cloud against a pale blue backdrop, the sky overhead now reflected larger, brighter patches of blue, and the sun, gaining strength, illuminated the countryside. As they neared the coast, glimpses of blue water slipped in between green and stone as the road they traveled snaked its way around curves, over hills, near the sea and then away.

Dunluce Castle first appeared as a stunning stone complex to the right of the road they drove along, disappearing from view as the road curved away. They pulled into a parking area, then walked the narrow path into the castle's complex.

While Maggie wandered around the entire complex, with its many arches, window openings, half ruined walls and intriguing turns, Bree was content to walk part of the grounds, choosing to spend most of her time staring into the Atlantic Ocean, mesmerized by the constant rolling waves, the many varied shades of blue, and the rhythm of wave and whitecap, whitecap and wave. The vastness of the body of water before her almost overwhelmed Bree. The closest she could get to that scale was Lake Erie, running along the Ohio coast, which she had visited when she'd traveled from her central Ohio home to Cleveland with friends several years back. She'd thought Lake Erie immense, but it paled in comparison to the endless stretch of water she gazed out upon now.

Grateful that she'd remembered to grab her good camera before heading out, Maggie took photo after photo of the various angles and openings the greyish tan stone walls of Dunluce offered. She captured images of a crow perching high atop a corner of a broken wall, and a wildflower growing through a gap in one of the stone edifices, its tiny, delicate pink petals cascading down the hard stone testament to its will to survive. She pondered the castle's history which they'd learned a bit about in the visitor center, and determined she would research it more deeply when she had time. Running her hands over the castle's walls, Maggie felt herself absorb the feeling of the stone's history into her heart, connecting so completely with the castle that it became a part of her, or she of it.

On their way back to the bed and breakfast, Bree received another text from Riley.

"Thanks Mom! Dad is making me and Regan spend our break with him! I can't believe you did this to us. I hate you!"

A wave of guilt as powerful as the windswept waves she had seen across the Atlantic washed over her. Setting aside her own feelings, she pictured Regan and Riley both home now, disappointed to be alone. Yes, they'd taken her for granted more times than they ever should have, and their failure to see or respond to her messages indicated they were more self-centered than they should be. If she put herself in their shoes though, she understood they were young and that the past few years had been more traumatic than either would admit.

Regan could brush off his feelings more easily and satisfy himself with camping and hiking, with his friends filling in where his father once had been. His natural carefree disposition overrode any hurt he carried inside him, or so Bree thought.

Riley, though, was another matter. For all her independent façade, for all her demanding ways, Bree knew she was still hurting inside over her parents' divorce and her father's abandonment of her in favor of his new family. She had been her daddy's girl ever since she was born, her world had been turned inside out and the wounds inside her cut deep. Being forced to spend time with their father would not be what either Regan or Riley would want; but only Riley would rail against it.

"Maybe I should book my flight home now," Bree mentioned as she and Maggie pulled into a free parking space behind the bed and breakfast. "Riley's very upset."

Maggie sent a raised eyebrow look back to her friend. "You're not serious, are you?"

"I don't know. They're both so unhappy, I don't think I can handle knowing their break isn't going the way they had wanted."

"Bree, they're twenty now. Time for them to look after themselves if you're away, and it's high time for you to start enjoying your life, without being on duty for them twenty-four/seven."

"Maggie, you wouldn't understand. You're not a mom." Catching the hurt that flashed across Maggie's face like lightning, there and gone in a second, Bree added, "I didn't say that to make you feel bad. You just don't know how it feels. My heart, my emotions, every part of me are tied to Regan and Riley in a way I can't explain. I've always been there for them, and I always will. This is the first time I've ever been away when they needed me."

"They don't need you, though." Maggie set aside the interior pain she felt whenever her lack of children surfaced. "They're independent enough to get by on their own when they're in college; they can fend for themselves now while you're away having what should be the time of your life."

Bree considered Maggie's words. "I know you're right, and of course I won't shorten my trip just because their plans have changed." Still, as Bree texted Regan and Riley to remind them she would be home in a matter of days, and their father was on hand to help with whatever they needed, part of her felt she was letting her children down.

Chapter Five

Allynwood Castle rose as a rectangular grey granite tower protruding from the soft green fields that surrounded it. Its grim, foreboding façade belied the grandeur that once filled its interior, as did the worn walls and furnishings that greeted visitors now. If visitors listened carefully, they might hear the echoes of laughter and music from dances and dinner parties Allynwood had been noted for in its heyday.

Built in the late 18th century, Allynwood Castle was at first home to Thomas and Jennie Allynwood and their young children. Having made his fortune in trading and supplying goods across Europe and beyond, Thomas was able to procure floor tiles from Italy, and silks from China and damask materials from the Middle East for curtains, tablecloths, and upholstery. For marble, though, Thomas chose Connemara marble, adorning fireplaces and columns with green, black, rose and white mottled variations of the stone quarried only in Ireland.

A large stained-glass window detailing the Allynwood family history was commissioned and installed at the first landing of the grand staircase with mahogany railings leading from the reception area on the first floor to the second and third floor bedrooms.

From its location half an hour southwest of Lough Neagh, Allynwood Castle looked out upon green fields and minor tributaries that fed into a small lough on the northwest corner of Allynwood's acreage. Workers were hired to take care of the flock of sheep that grazed the fields and the horses Thomas and Jennie and their children rode, the various crops raised to either market or feed the Allynwoods and nearby townspeople, and the elaborate gardens of herbs, vegetables, and various flower specimens. The rose garden at Allynwood was famous throughout the region for its varieties and their well cared for beauty.

Their oldest son, Thomas Jr., inherited Allynwood when Thomas Sr. passed, and passed it to Thomas III when his turn to leave came around. Thomas III, however, frequently given to gambling beyond his means, let the castle fall into disrepair. He died early; some credited his death to too much drink while others suspected those to whom he owed money had a hand in his passing.

Thomas III's married sister, Annie Doyle, being the sole survivor of Thomas Allynwood's family, inherited the castle. It remained in Allynwood-Doyle family hands, but its once famous glory was never restored.

JACKSON "Jax" Doyle raised himself from the ground where he had been laying stone for a new pathway, arched his back to ease some of its soreness, and brushed dirt away from the knees of his worn jeans. He surveyed the work he'd done so far that morning, then eyed the grounds surrounding the castle. Everywhere he looked, he saw so much that needed care. The flower gardens that lined the back patio were in a shambles and would need a complete overhaul, rhododendron and azalea specimens that had been planted along the east and west edges of the lawn bore yellowed, spotted leaves and would need consistent feeding to bring them back to their former beauty. Broken cement on patio steps and the pathways encircling the castle needed replacing. The vegetable gardens and herb garden would have to be re-established, and the rose garden Allynwood was noted for would take months, if not years, to restore.

And that was just the outside! Inside, the castle needed so much updating and refurbishing Jax didn't know where to begin. In the eighteen months since he'd inherited Allynwood, he had tried to work out a master plan for bringing the castle up to par, but every month some new repair threw his plan into disarray.

MAGGIE decided the best place to start with the list of repairs the cottage needed was to obtain estimates for the work beyond her ability to handle, and supplies for the parts she could manage herself. Painting interior walls would be easy, but there was little use in taking that on until ceiling cracks could be plastered and ceilings painted, which might as well wait until roof leaks were patched. Online searches for cupboard, counter and sink replacement yielded price estimates, but the most reasonable repairmen in price were booked for the next two months.

After days of research and frustration, Maggie told Bree, "I'm glad you booked that castle for us! I could do with a break!"

Allynwood Castle didn't look much like Maggie had expected as she and Bree pulled onto the grounds for their overnight stay. While the photos Bree had shown her revealed a dull exterior, Maggie was taken aback to find the stones darker grey than she'd anticipated. With only one other car in the graveled car park, a deep sense of isolation swept over Maggie; a sign posted at the end of the car park which read "Park At Your Own Risk" further unsettled her.

"Are you sure this is where we want to spend the night?"

Bree surveyed the exterior with the same sense of foreboding, noting a loose gutter along one side of the roof, cracks in one of the first-floor windows, and a torn entryway flag. She checked her phone, confirmed they were in the right location and replied, "It doesn't look this run down in its website photos, but let's go in and give it a chance."

Inside, the narrow castle entry steps opened up to a large central room with stone walls, worn tiled floor, a seating area with a sofa and three armchairs, and a massive fireplace with carved marble sides and a marble mantel. Suspended from the high ceiling were two circular wrought iron chandeliers with candle shaped bulbs. Maggie imagined by night the bulbs would create a soft glow reminiscent of what a true candle chandelier would have afforded back in the day. Maybe the low light would hide some of the flaws and provide guests with a sense of the charm the castle once held.

The bedroom they were directed to was austere by castle standards, with twin beds, a single antique dresser with curved mirror, an armchair next to the window near the dresser, and an en suite bathroom with the bare minimum number of towels.

Bree lowered herself onto the edge of the twin bed nearest the door. "Not the glamour we expected, is it?"

Sharing her friend's disappointment but not wanting to make Bree feel worse, Maggie tried to find a positive side. "Still, we're in a castle, and to be honest this might be more authentic than one of those glitzy renovated luxury hotel type places."

"Maybe." Bree let Maggie's words ease her regret. "Well, anyway, we're here and the sun has broken through this morning's clouds; let's go explore the grounds before another round of rain moves in."

Starting with the front walkway, they strolled along the castle ground's perimeter, past tall trees that lined either side of the lawns, admiring the rhododendron and azalea groves and holly, hydrangea and wild berry shrubs that graced the trees' lower regions. At a corner of the grounds where a stand of birch trees stood guard, a small lough appeared.

"Look how the sunlight plays off the water," Maggie commented. "If I lived here, I'd want to come out every sunrise and sunset and watch how the water's colors change."

Where the perimeter of Allynwood's grounds appeared well cared for, at least to Maggie and Bree's unprofessional eyes, as they drew closer to the castle itself they could see how whatever gardens had once graced the courtyard had deteriorated.

"That's not all that's fallen apart." Bree pointed to broken concrete on the back stairs, and cracks in the stone walls that separated the patio garden from the expanse of lawn beyond it. "Between the gardens and the masonry repairs, this place needs more work than your cottage does!"

Maggie groaned. "Don't remind me about the cottage! I'm trying to not think about it!"

They hurried inside as raindrops returned. Maggie and Bree spent the afternoon in the drawing room watching raindrops splash against the windows, sipping tea and savoring scones, trying to imagine what life in the castle at the height of its grandeur would have been like.

"Imagine the women with all their silks and jewelry, sipping tea like we are, or overseeing large dinner parties." As she spoke, Bree pictured women with long, rustling dresses strolling through gardens, relaxing in the drawing room, or seated at long tables adorned with fine china and sparkling crystal.

The contrast between Allynwood's once stately past and the small cottage her ancestors had lived in was not lost on Maggie. "I wonder if the owners were kind to their staff, or if they were harsh landowners."

Maggie and Bree noticed more of the castle's deficiencies as they dined that evening.

Bree pointed to a broken windowpane near their table in the castle's dining room. "Their website failed to post that photo! It doesn't look like that break is new, look at all the grime covering it, and the spiderwebs! It's been broken a while."

Maggie couldn't stifle her laugh. "If you were trying to draw guests to stay at your place, you'd leave that photo out!"

Engrossed in their conversation, neither Bree nor Maggie noticed the man behind the dining room's bar taking note of their comments. Working as bartender and waiter since Marty, who had been hired for those roles, had called in sick, Jax couldn't help overhearing Bree and Maggie as they were the only guests dining in. As aware as he was of the many improvements Allynwood needed, he still listened to what the girls were saying. He would later check their comments against the list of needed repairs he had already drawn up.

He was there again the next morning as Maggie and Bree talked over breakfast.

"You're good at interior design." Maggie waved a hand through the air around them. "What would you do different here?"

Bree studied the dining room. Daylight showed details she had missed the night before, cracks in several spots in the ceiling plaster, worn patches in two corners of the rug. Flaws aside, though, she found the room's spaciousness appealing, freeing something inside her she didn't know how to put into words, as if a wide window had opened into a soul that had been closed off far too long.

"I'd start with fixing the windowpane, the cracks in the walls, update the carpet, and give the walls a fresh coat of paint. In fact, the whole place needs updating, although I'd want to retain as much of the furniture as I could to keep the historical element intact."

Maggie persisted, "But if you could, if you had a free hand here, how would you redecorate?"

"The entranceway," Bree announced, staring past Maggie as if she could see the reception area guests first walked into upon arriving at the castle. "The sofa and chairs there need reupholstering, and it should be given a much grander look, something that showcases that glorious fireplace!"

"That fireplace is amazing, isn't it?" Maggie pictured again the intricate carvings that had been worked into the marble that framed the fireplace, and the wide grey, green and white veined marble mantel upon which sat two brass candlesticks and a clock. "I'd love to see how you could transform this castle."

"I'd be interested to see that too."

Bree and Maggie both jumped at the voice that had come up behind them.

"My name is Jackson, Jax to my friends. I do most of the maintenance work around here. I heard you talking last night and again just now about what you would do to improve our place. I don't know how long you're staying here, but I'd love to talk to you more about renovations."

Whether the light in Jax's green eyes drew her in, or the stubble along his jawline as if he hadn't had time to shave in days, Bree couldn't tell; but she felt her pulse racing at a pace it hadn't moved in years. Not sure she liked or trusted the feeling, she forced herself to take slow breaths and focus on one of the fleur-de-lis designs on the drapery behind him as she replied, "I doubt I know enough about renovating castles to be of much help."

Jax smiled to himself at the sudden flush in her cheeks. She intrigued him.

It had been years since a girl had stirred inside him such a powerful desire to find out more about her. "I disagree. You've already picked up on some of our immediate needs. I heard your friend here say you know interior design; I'd like to show you around our building and grounds and get some more input from you."

Bree glanced at Maggie as if to ask, "Should I?" Maggie offered back an almost imperceptible shrug of her shoulders, unsure if Bree was seeking permission or a way out.

Sometimes a once in a lifetime opportunity comes a person's way. Sometimes one must take a chance, no matter how crazy it seems. Bree knew this. She'd wanted some kind of adventure on this trip. Now one presented itself; she knew she'd hate herself if she passed this opportunity up.

"My friend and I are due to check out of the castle by noon. I'm not sure I can offer much advice, but if you'd like to give me a tour of the place, I'll give you whatever advice I can."

"I would appreciate that." Jax nodded towards the hallway that led to the reception area. "Take your time finishing your meal. I'll be by the front desk when you're ready."

"You go ahead," Maggie told Bree after Jax had left. "Let him show you the property. I still have calls to repairmen to make, and plenty to keep me occupied."

Bree shot a suspicious look Maggie's way. "You're doing it again, trying to set me up, trying to spark something between me and whatever handsome man is within radar. There's nothing to spark here, it's just a stroll through the building and gardens. Come with us."

"I'm not setting you up," Maggie protested, although in her heart she would be happy to see Bree meet someone better than the ex-husband who had betrayed her best friend, someone deserving of Bree's kind, trusting heart. "He'll want to hear more of your thoughts on how to improve the place. I'll be a distraction."

Despite Bree's further urgings, Maggie held her ground, requested a second cup of tea and stayed behind. Bree met Jax in the reception area and followed as he led her through the castle. In addition to twenty-four en suite bedrooms, and an upstairs sitting area where guests could find a quiet place to read or meditate, the castle included the first floor drawing area she and Maggie had enjoyed the afternoon before in addition to the relaxing soft chairs and sofa in the reception area, and a first floor kitchen. A tour of the basement revealed a prep kitchen where, in earlier times, game would have been prepared over the large stone fireplace along with various stews and side dishes, shelves where preserved foods would have been stored, and four small rooms where servants would have slept.

Stepping outside then, Bree and Jax found the overnight rain had subsided and a weak sun was trying to push its way through a layer of clouds. The back patio Bree had spotted the day before, surrounded by perennial flowers and ivy struggling to survive, gave way to an expanse of lawn dotted with what once would have been more formal gardens.

"This was a kitchen garden." Jax pointed to an area on the left. "Chefs back in the day would have grown vegetables and herbs here to use in preparing meals. I want to re-establish that, but I have a lot to learn about growing vegetables and herbs. I also would love to someday see a greenhouse installed for growing fruits and indoor plants."

Leading farther over the grounds, Jax showed Bree a rose garden beyond the kitchen garden site that showed signs of re-design work, a perennial garden on the right in bad need of weeding, and a lavender garden where a rusted white wrought iron table and four rusted chairs had been abandoned.

"This was the tea garden," Jax told Bree. "Ladies would read here or work on painting, all very upper class, refined."

"Your guests would probably enjoy having that restored. You could add another table and chairs, or maybe a matching table and chairs somewhere in the perennial garden opposite here."

"Put that in your notes, please," Jax advised. "That would draw guests outside."

Standing at the edge of the lawn, Jax pointed beyond the grass to the wooded areas behind the castle. "Our property extends about a hundred acres beyond this. I've long thought an arboretum, a collection of specimen shrubs and trees, would be grand. I'm not sure it can be done, but if you could add that to the list I'd be grateful." He turned to Bree then. "I imagine the list you're building is rather long, and possibly beyond the resources available to upgrade this place."

Bree scanned the gardens and grounds and turned back to look at the castle. Broken windows in the stone shed at the end of a wall adjoining it to the back of the castle needed replacing, and some of the stones along the arched wall appeared loose. Inside, she'd seen further evidence of frayed, worn rugs, curtains, and bed coverings, faded walls, and light fixtures that at the very least could use a good polishing. If funds were no issue, she could envision a complete overhaul and grand, coordinated design. Jax had hinted at limited resources though; and Bree chose a more scaled down approach.

"I'd have to give this more thought," she told him, "but I think the castle could at least get away with a face lift, not too pricey, just some proper attention paid to it."

As they stepped back inside, Bree admired with a fresh view the central room that had at some point become the reception area. She once again felt a hint of the castle's former glory whispering to her through the walls, through the fireplace, through the arched windows, just as it had while Jax had shown her the castle's various rooms, and as it had more loudly through the gardens and grounds. There was something here worth saving, she knew, something worth bringing back to life.

"This room should have two things," she suggested, sweeping her hand around the room they stood in. "Something that gives visitors a sense of the castle's history, and some touch of elegance, of the specialness of entering a castle. It's not, after all, like any other hotel guests are entering. If you can find out for me how much the owners are willing to spend on refurbishing, I'll draft a plan for you."

"Will do." Jax avoided the receptionist's quizzical glance. "How can I reach you?"

On a piece of paper the receptionist handed to her, Bree wrote her cell phone number. "You can call or text me here. Maggie and I are staying near Gaffney for about another week."

"Right. Thank you. I should be in touch by tomorrow."

After Bree and Maggie had gone upstairs to gather their belongings and prepare for checking out, Colleen, the receptionist, turned to Jax.

"You didn't tell her you're the owner?"

Jax turned his eyes from the staircase Bree had ascended to the girl behind the desk. "No, and don't you tell her."

"I won't, but why the secret?"

"It just complicates things." What Jax didn't say, what he kept to himself, was that he found Bree quite enticing, his heart was drawn to her in a way it hadn't been drawn in years. He had little time, though, to dwell on that. His phone buzzed: another call from a developer who had tried every day in the past week to reach him. Jax knew what the developer wanted and answered the call if only to get the caller off his back.

"Andrew, what can I do for you?"

"Same as I always want. My backers are interested in your property."

"You know it's not for sale."

"You know you can't put it off forever. You're in dire straits there."

An involuntary deep inhale left all Jax's muscles tight. "I'm not so bad off I can't turn things around."

Andrew softened his tone. "You're still young, Jackson. Why saddle yourself with the never-ending burden of keeping up a castle that will be a constant financial drain, possibly even bankrupt you. You know my people have endless resources and can turn your property into a five-star luxury destination. Why not let us take the burden off your shoulders and give Allynwood the kind of showplace look it deserves?"

"Thank you for your compassion," Jax replied, feeling anything but grateful. "My answer is still no." With that, he terminated the call.

Turning to Colleen, knowing she'd heard his end of the call, Jax confided, "If we don't make some real improvements here, we risk losing this place. Developers are constantly reaching out to me. I know what they want: to strip my home of its unique character and turn it into a carbon copy luxury resort. If it takes everything I have to turn this castle around and make it a proper draw for visitors, I'll do it. I know the odds are against me. I know it may drive me under. But I love this place; my heritage is here, my blood flows through these walls. I can't just let it go."

Chapter Six

"Maggie? Sean McCabe here. You've had a few days to check out the cottage; I was just wondering how you're getting on."

Maggie turned from the list of roofing contractors she had pulled up on her laptop. "I'm getting along alright, thank you. The cottage is very pretty, although as you said it needs a few repairs."

"Are you planning to take them on yourself? Or have you given thought to foregoing your inheritance?"

"I still have a few weeks to make my decision, don't I?"

"Yes, you do."

Maggie thought again of the property the father she'd never known had left her. "I have to admit, it's a hard choice to make. I'm sure this sounds crazy, but I feel a connection to the place I can't explain."

Sean nodded to himself, aware that Maggie could not see his reaction through the phone lines. "That's not crazy at all," he reassured her. "It's not uncommon for people with Irish ancestry to feel an unexpected connection when they arrive here."

Maggie gave a light laugh. "It's good to know I'm not losing my mind! As for the cottage, the most immediate repair is on the roof, I can see where there have been a few leaks. I'm having a hard time finding anyone who has the time to come out and inspect it. Would you be able to recommend a good roofer?"

"Yes, let me check my contacts and get back to you." A thought occurred to Sean and he added, "If you'd like to know more about the place and your family's history, you might try to contact Liam McAllister. I'll get you his number as well; the easiest place to reach him is at Oxford Island Nature Reserve, it's not too far from here. He's our local expert on the history of most of the family lines in these parts."

Two hours later, Maggie had booked an appointment with Gareth McManus to provide an estimate for roofing repairs and was on her way to meet with Liam McAllister.

Maggie had no trouble locating the nature reserve, a fifteen-minute drive from town, and was taken in by the beauty of its surroundings as she walked towards the entrance. Birds fluttered and chirped among a stand of pines to the right. A nature trail wound its way through wildflowers and shrubs to the left. The center itself, painted white and tan to blend in with the scattering of birch trees planted around it, was fitted with tall, wide windows to afford visitors full views of the lough behind and natural growth all around. Ducks quacked and splashed in a small pond by the bridge that led to the entrance, and a wind chime sent soft notes through the gentle breeze.

"Is Liam McAllister here?" She asked the young woman behind the desk.

"Let me check. Is he expecting you?"

"Yes. Please tell him Maggie McCarey is here."

Moments later, Liam rounded the corner and greeted her. "My office is this way," he motioned to a hallway behind him. "Can I get you some tea and biscuits?"

"Tea would be nice, thank you."

Liam motioned for them to sit at a rectangular low table set in front of a wide window, with the nature reserve's lough in full view.

"That's lovely," Maggie commented as she took her seat. "I'd have a hard time focusing on work with a view like that."

"It isn't easy," Liam agreed. "Thankfully, my job has me outdoors much more than in, so I don't mind letting go of the view from time to time."

He opened a folder and withdrew a printout. "You asked me to research your family history, and in particular anything I could find on your property. You said you had no information at all regarding your family name, is that correct?"

"Yes. My mother recently passed, I only found out about the cottage I've inherited and the family connection after she was gone."

Liam nodded with understanding. "I'm sorry for your loss. I was able to pull together two reports for you. One is a record of your ancestral line from the 1700s to when your great-great-grandfather emigrated in the late 1850s. I was then able to research American immigration records and trace your line to present day, to Hugh, who I believe was your father, is that correct?"

"Yes." Maggie received the first report Liam handed her, feeling as if he was giving her paperwork worth its weight in gold.

"Look this over at your leisure. If you have any questions, you can always get in touch with me." Liam settled back in his chair and read from a second printout. "This is the history of your property. Your great-great-grandfather, Nathaniel, constructed the cottage I would estimate around 1830, most likely at the direction of the landowner he worked for. He would have rented the cottage for a number of years, until he had enough funds to purchase the cottage outright. Over time it has passed through several hands but always remained in your family. Nathaniel's descendants not only retained possession, over the years they have added onto it and appear to have maintained it well until recently. Your father would have been the last owner."

Maggie received this report from Liam as well. "I can't believe you found this much information so fast! You've given me much more than I hoped for. I've gone from having no clue at all about my Irish roots to having a family tree and the start of understanding what the cottage might have meant to my ancestors."

Liam sized up the woman sitting across from him. Maggie carried about her an air of wisdom and self assurance. While he didn't know her back story, he could imagine the shock she would have felt in finding out about a heritage she'd had no knowledge of. The fact that she cared enough to want to learn about her ancestors, rather than just brush them aside, impressed him.

"I'm sure learning you have Irish ancestry was a great surprise for you. These reports are a good starting point. You may want to learn more about Irish and Northern Irish history, as they're so interconnected, get to know some of the music and traditions. If you ever have any questions along those lines, you can always ask me. Do you have any idea what you'll do with the property you've inherited?"

Maggie confessed, "To be honest, at first I thought I would fly over here, review the property, sell it, and return home. Now, I'm not so sure. I've kind of fallen in love with the place, with the town it's near, with the whole countryside. I think I need to give myself more time to decide."

Liam turned his most serious look Maggie's way. "I hope you will retain the property in your family. Many of the cottages from that time period have disappeared, eroded through time, weather, and lack of attention. For all that your ancestors managed to battle their way through to keep that cottage, it would be a shame to lose it now."

Maggie watched as a white swan flew in from the right and settled upon the lough's blue waters. It splashed in then floated, preening its feathers a bit before settling, content to bob along the rippled surface. Drawn to its buoyancy, Maggie thought of her own life, the times her own waters were smooth and she floated along undisturbed, the times winds blew and caused minor ripples to grow into larger waves that were difficult to navigate. She admired how easily the swan floated, and wondered if now, facing the highest waves she'd ever faced, she would be able to ride the waters unfazed as this swan did.

As she watched the swans, she reflected on what Liam had revealed to her about how old the cottage was that had come her way, how long it had been in her family's possession. She felt again the pull of something drawing her to this new corner of the world, some internal magnet connecting her feet to ground they had never stepped on before. Sean McCabe had called it genetic memory, imprints on one's body's cells passed down from ancestors whether one had known them or not.

Maggie thought again of the dream she had carried inside her for more years than she could remember. Bree had mentioned it when Maggie lost her job. She'd thought of it as she spent time in the cottage her father had left her.

What if, instead of turmoil, all the recent events in her life were conspiring to point her life in a new direction?

She felt an impulse to disclose her idea to Liam and followed the urge. "I was thinking this is an opportunity to follow a dream I've had for years. I'd like to open a bookstore in the larger room of the cottage and use the rest as my residence. My guess is most people in Gaffney travel to Lurgan to buy books, or order them online, but a small bookstore within easy reach might be appealing."

"McCarey blood runs through you indeed," Liam replied, face beaming. "Determined, and a bit of a dreamer. I like that!" He considered her idea. "A small bookstore might work. If you include books by local authors that would appeal to some around you." Then he cautioned, "Tread slowly, Maggie. People in this area are distrustful of strangers at first. Our history is complex. Don't discuss politics or religion, and don't run too far ahead with your plans. Give people time to get to know you. Even the idea of a bookshop, small and unthreatening as it may be, might not be welcomed with open arms at first."

Maggie turned his advice over in her mind, storing it away for the days and weeks ahead. Gathering the printouts he had provided, she rose and shook Liam's hand. "Thank you so much for all your research work. Do I owe you anything for your services?"

Liam smiled back. "Nothing at all, I was happy to do this. If you'd ever like a tour of our grounds here, I'd be glad to show you around. I wish you good fortune with your endeavors. Please keep me posted."

Watching as Maggie left the visitor center, got into her car and drove away, Liam thought again what an intriguing woman she was. Poised on the brink of following a dream, she showed no fear, only the slightest hesitation as to whether her course was right.

His own dream rose once again from the corner of his heart where he'd locked it away so many years ago. He had always wanted to become a wood carver. Oh, he knew he'd never make a living at the craft, but he so admired the carvings of other crafters he'd seen, and each time something stirred deep inside him. He had taken a few classes, loved the feel of wood in his hands, and the process of cutting deep grooves in some places, or forming raised designs in others, loved how a block of wood could be shaped and transformed so a bird rose out of it, or a sheep, or a flower.

Then he'd married, and he and Brigid had had a son, Kevin, and a daughter, Elaine. Raising a family and holding down a full-time job managing a local market left little time for wood carving, although from time to time he would pick up his tools and fashion a toy for his children or a gift for his wife.

Kevin had died in a boating accident while in secondary school. Elaine married and moved to Australia; he received an occasional card from her but nothing more.

For their thirtieth anniversary, Brigid had presented him with a new, more professional set of carving tools, and urged him to pursue the craft once again. Six months later she'd been diagnosed with breast cancer, two years later she was gone. The tools had been set aside; he had not since entered the shed he'd long ago made his workshop.

Liam had seen the way Maggie's face had lit up when she mentioned her dream of converting her family's cottage into a bookstore. In that one brief exchange something inside her sprang to life. As she spoke, a spark had also been lit inside him, which caught fire as he now watched her drive away. Returning to his office, he promised himself that when he went home that night he would pull out his carving tools and once again reach for his dream.

BREE studied the notes she had taken while Jax toured Allynwood with her, and envisioned once again the castle, gloomy on the outside but with so much potential for light and beauty inside. When Jax had asked her to provide some input as to how the castle's interior could be improved, outwardly she had played it cool while inside her heart was so excited she wondered that it hadn't burst!

Interior design had always been the great, unrealized passion in her life. She remembered how it had started; she was seven when her parents had given her a proper dollhouse and miniature doll family to play with. Oh, the dolls were fine, but the most fun she had was in fitting out the various rooms in the dollhouse. As she'd grown older the dolls had disappeared, stored away in some box or other in her closet, but the dollhouse she'd transformed over and over, changing out rugs and furniture, and painting, papering or stenciling walls. Testing out one color scheme after another, one arrangement and then another, she found more joy in the dollhouse than in any other toy or game she received over the years.

Progressing to high school, as she considered what path her life would take beyond graduation, Bree returned time and again to the idea of interior decorating as a career. It seemed a natural direction; she constantly had an eye on how rooms were decorated, whether in movie scenes, magazine displays, or visiting the houses of family and friends. Her opinions and suggestions were asked more and more when friends or family were giving their rooms a face lift; each time the thrill of color and arrangement increased in her, confirming this was the clear path for her life.

Bree started college, was a year and a half into it when she met Carter, a fellow student whose focus was on business management. Oh, she'd fallen hard for him! He looked like a young George Hamilton with his dark hair, dark eyes, and riveting gaze. Half the girls on campus were drawn to him. When she was the one he'd asked out, other girls scorned her but she didn't care! She'd won the prize! She hadn't minded when marriage and motherhood derailed her interior decorating dreams, she was following something so much more satisfying.

Now, as she considered how best to approach Allynwood's needs, she felt she was in over her head. Having a good eye for decorating hers and several friends' houses was a great deal different than providing ideas for a centuries old castle.

Feeling the need to take a break from her mental torment, Bree called Riley. "Hi honey, how are you and your brother getting on?"

There was no mistaking the anger underlying Riley's response. "A lot you care!"

"Don't be like that," Bree ordered. "Of course I care. Are you still at your father's house?"

"We're here, but we'd rather be home. All he cares about is his new family!"

"Did you give him a chance? Or did you go there with a lot of attitude?"

"I've been on my best behavior!"

Bree recognized the sarcasm in Riley's statement. Not that she could blame her daughter. In Riley's place, Bree would have carried attitude as well.

"When are you coming home, Mom?"

Bree drew a deep breath before she replied, sure her daughter would not like what she heard. "I'm not sure yet, but not before you return to college next week."

Riley hung up without another word and Bree felt another bout of failure as a mother. She'd already failed as a wife. Turning once again to her castle repair notes, Bree vowed to herself she would not fail at this task.

Gareth McManus came out the next morning, inspected the cottage's slate roof condition and reported to Maggie, "Your roof has several broken tiles and gaps between tiles where water is getting in. I would replace the entire roof, which would cost more than you want to spend unless you're going to keep the house and move in." At Maggie's surprised look, he explained, "I do a lot of business in Gaffney. It's a small town, people talk, word spreads fast. I know you've inherited this place. If you'd rather I can patch the roof, but any new owner will run into problems over time."

"Could you provide me estimates for both the roof replacement and the smaller repair job? I'll need to think over the best way to handle this."

"A whole roof?" Bree gave Maggie a surprised look as Maggie related Gareth's words to her. "Well, the estimates you get back might help you decide whether you're going to keep this place or sell it."

"I think I already know which way I'm leaning. I just want to turn it over in my mind a little longer."

Maggie remembered Liam's words advising her, no, fairly ordering her, to preserve what Nathaniel had built and her ancestors had treasured. Running her hands over countertops and along door frames, she imagined how many times they had touched the same surfaces. She was sure their footsteps echoed her own as she wandered from room to room envisioning how she could dress each one up. She thought she could hear their voices whispering to her through the air inside the walls.

Stepping outside, she walked the boundaries of the property surrounding the cottage. Had her ancestors grown vegetables here, and should she do the same? How could she restore the front courtyard into a welcoming green space? What flowers would mirror what they might have grown? Had Nathaniel planted any of the nearby trees? What stars would shine down on her here, and had her ancestors studied them the way she hoped to?

Maggie pictured the condo she currently lived in, and the apartment her mother had left behind. She remembered the job she'd just been released from, and that she'd have to find another place of employment when she returned home. If she returned home. The idea of returning to Ohio almost repulsed her. Northern Ireland had not only gotten under her skin, it had called her home. She'd have to work through whatever process was involved to extend her visa, then to file for whatever permits were needed for her to stay here. Her long-suppressed dream of opening a small bookstore suddenly was within reach. Fear rattled her nerves a bit as she considered the possibility of finally risking everything to follow her dream. Never one to take risks, she was about to step out on the biggest risk ever.

"Maybe I'm crazy," she confided to the oak at the back corner of her land. "What if I can't pull this all off? What if I sink all my money into renovation and stocking of a small collection of books and no one supports it? I could lose all I own on this! There's no safety net underneath me; I could completely go under chasing after a childhood dream! Am I out of my mind?"

A sudden rustle of leaves on the oak tree startled her. No other trees or plants stirred. Maggie had an odd sensation the tree had heard her and was answering, whispering in its own way that she wasn't crazy, that she was indeed of very sound mind, and that any dream was worth pursuing if one wanted it badly enough.

Before stepping back inside to where Bree waited, Maggie whispered to the oak and to any of her ancestors whose spirits might be within earshot, "I'm going to give this my all. Please let my efforts succeed."

Bree saw a new look on Maggie's face when she returned, an assurance Bree hadn't seen there in quite some time. "You've made your mind up, haven't you."

"I have. I'm going to keep this place, turn it into a small bookstore. You know I've always dreamed of that!"

Bree sank into the sitting room chair, stunned. "Are you saying you'd move here permanently?"

"What do I have to go back to?"

"Me, for one!"

Maggie sat down across from Bree and reached for her friend's hand. "I don't want to leave you. You're my best friend. But a door has been opened for me, and I think I have to take it! If I didn't, I'd always wonder if I could have done this."

Bree still resisted. "You know this isn't real, don't you?" Bree could always gauge Maggie's mindset by the look in her eyes; right now, Maggie's eyes shone with such an intensity of blue they were almost the same as the ocean. "Dream living is visiting a place and believing you could stay there forever. Real is a job, responsibilities, and the place you build your home."

"Real is my mother's death, having no job to go home to, no family ties to hold me anyplace," Maggie countered. Feeling her life looked and sounded pathetic, Maggie turned on Bree to deflect attention away from herself. "Real is a husband who has an affair with a young office worker and walks out on his wife and children. Real is children who use their mother as chef, laundress, and money bank. Real is …".

"Alright," Bree broke in. "I get the picture! Anything, even imaginary lives, would look better than what we both have waiting for us back home. Still, you're talking about upending everything for a dream whose chance for success is slim at best."

"I know. Well, I won't sell my condo just yet. I'll keep it in case my plans fall through."

With her decision made, Maggie's next step was to meet with Sean McCabe and finalize her inheritance.

"I've decided to keep the property," she informed him. "You mentioned there would be papers for me to sign."

"Yes, I have them all prepared for you." Sean pulled out his McCarey folder, described each piece of paper as he handed it to her, and indicated where she needed to sign.

"There are some financial items to discuss," he then told her, setting an itemized statement before her. "In managing your father's estate, there were some expenditures I paid out with respect to the property, taxes, utility bills and the like. It's all listed here. I've also itemized the finances your father left behind, minus what I advanced to pay his various expenses, and what remains in his account. As you can see, there's very little money left."

Maggie reviewed the itemization and figures, satisfied that everything seemed in order. "Thank you for this, for everything you've done." She hesitated, debating within herself whether she should disclose all her plans to Sean. In the end, she knew she might need help from him to navigate the process of opening a business here. "I might need your assistance on something else, if you're willing. I'd like to open a small bookstore in the cottage. Do you foresee any problems with that?"

Sean studied the woman before him. She was hardly the naïve young woman who had entered his office days ago, unsure whether she would even keep the cottage her father had left her. Now she sat here not only signing the papers needed to finalize her inheritance, but also announcing her plans to stay in the country and open a new business. She was a determined one, he thought.

He also realized Patrick would not be happy to learn Maggie intended to keep the property.

Chapter Seven

Excited when he received the call from Sean to come to his office, Patrick let his mind run far ahead with plans for the cottage he was sure would now be his. The property's close proximity to Gaffney, Lurgan, and many of Northern Ireland's tourist attractions would make it very appealing to travelers seeking a modest, reasonably priced accommodation. He would give each of the rooms a fresh coat of paint, spruce up the kitchen a bit, purchase new bedding and towels, and start offering the cottage for short-term rentals within a month. As he drove to Gaffney, Patrick's mind had already started running through ideas for how he would word advertisements offering the cottage and choosing which tourism companies he would contact first to get them on board with spreading word of the cottage's availability.

So certain was he that the cottage would come into his possession, he was in no way prepared for Sean's news.

"The American lass is going to keep the cottage."

"What?" Aware he had shouted the word, Patrick sat back down in the chair he had leapt up from, and repeated in a lowered voice, "What?"

Sean told him again, "Maggie has decided she wants to keep the cottage, maybe turn it into a bookstore."

"She can't do that!"

"I'm sorry to say, she can."

"It's not fair! She didn't even know about the cottage until a week ago. She didn't know anything about her father! Hugh wasn't even in touch with her! Why would he leave it to her and not to proper family he's known all his life?"

Sean could only shrug. "Maybe it was his way of making amends somehow."

"That's a shite reason! What do I have to do to protest his will? Sure, the property belongs in the hands of a proper citizen, not some foreigner!"

"Technically, she's not a foreigner. She's a UK citizen by way of her father being one. Patrick, I've double checked all aspects of her inheritance. Hugh's will was properly written and filed, Maggie is within her rights in claiming it. There's nothing more you can do."

"But I had plans for that place!"

Sean felt for the man seated before him. He knew Patrick well, had seen all the times and ways Patrick's life had taken bad turns. Whatever Patrick's plans were, now they had fallen through, and Sean could not help but feel sorry for him.

Still, Maggie was within her legal rights, the will was valid and unassailable, and Sean knew Patrick well enough to caution him, "Don't be causing any trouble for the American now. The property is hers; you need to let it all go and let her do as she wishes with it."

BITTERNESS raged inside Patrick as he complained to his best friend, Tim. "I'm telling ye, they've got it all wrong, the place should have gone to me! It were stolen from me!"

Trying to console his friend, Tim placed a hand on Patrick's arm. "I don't think it was stolen. You just didn't plan on Hugh leaving the place to anyone else. You got your hopes up too high is all."

"In all these years I never heard Hugh mention a daughter. She never came over here to see him. The family hardly even remembered he had a daughter across the pond. In all the months since he passed, we never heard a word from her. If she'd stayed away a bit longer, his place would have been mine!"

"She did appear, though."

"Ah, but the dreams I had, Tim! I were going to dress the place up fine, make it shine, turn it into a grand bed and breakfast! It were my one chance to raise a right proper business, something I could be proud of instead of always feeling a failure."

How many times had Tim heard Patrick recite his dreams, list the various plans he had, the steps he'd take to turn the aging cottage into a viable business? Sure, Patrick's dreams were all wrapped up in one outcome, one slim hope that he might be granted the property after Hugh had passed. They were not foolish hopes either, Tim had to agree. The cottage had been left empty long enough, half the town assumed Patrick would eventually be granted title to it. Maggie's sudden appearance led most of them to understand Patrick's dream was over. Patrick was the only one who still carried the delusion inside him.

"Your idea was a grand one," Tim agreed now. "Maybe you could find another place to renovate; there's sure to be some in nearby towns or the countryside."

"Aye, and at a grand price! This one would have been mine free and clear. You know I don't have the money for other places!"

Having experienced his own share of dreams shattering over time, Tim understood his friend's disappointment now. Still, there was nothing for it but to put it behind him and move on with life. He tried to persuade Patrick of the same. "You've lost the inheritance, sure. It's over. Time to let the cottage go."

"Not yet it's not!" Patrick vowed. The fire in his friend's eyes made Tim wonder what plans could now be churning in Patrick's mind.

BREE once again scanned through the cell phone photos of Allynwood Castle she had taken as she had toured the building and grounds with Jax, comparing them with various interior photos of other Irish castles she had collected from the internet.

Some of the castles she studied focused on the grandeur of earlier times in which the castles had been built for wealthy landowners, decorating their interiors with expensive fabrics and draperies, elegant accommodations for guests, and photo lined hallways that celebrated the elite who in times past had graced the castle grounds.

Other castles focused on medieval histories, displaying armor, weapons, and rudimentary furnishings that seemed too stark to appeal to overnight guests.

Then there were castles who had sacrificed their uniqueness to become wedding destination locations and their interior decorating styles, while maintaining some sense of individuality, all seemed similar enough that she found it hard to differentiate which castle was which.

She hoped Allynwood would never become that kind of castle.

Trying to get a sense of the particular style that would best suit Allynwood's history and rural setting, Bree settled on two themes: focusing on its closeness to and love of nature, and displaying whatever the owners would agree to of the castle's historical artifacts. Of the several she and Maggie had noticed, the mounted heads of deer and game the castle's ancestors had shot were her least favorite. Maybe Jax could persuade the owners to relocate those trophies to private quarters; not every guest staying at Allynwood would appreciate their value.

By lunchtime, Bree had assembled sufficient notes and website links to be prepared whenever Jax requested to meet with her.

As Bree researched and planned out Allynwood Castle's improvements, Maggie continued phone calls with repairmen to schedule estimates and work to bring the cottage, her cottage, up to proper condition. After completing her calls, Maggie stood in the cottage's central room and visualized once again how she would set it up as a bookstore. In her mind's eye, she planned out where she would install shelves, what they would look like lined with various books' colorful spines, where a second easy chair would be placed next to the first one to encourage conversation or quiet reading, and whether the low table in the center of the room should be kept, or replaced with a more modern one. She decided the current one would do, at least for now. In the kitchen off to the right she could brew tea for any patrons who wanted some, and perhaps keep on hand a plate of the shortbread she had become known for making for friends and co-workers each Christmas.

Early afternoon arrived, announced by pangs of hunger that forced Maggie to check the time.

"Are you at a good stopping point for lunch?" she called out to Bree. "I thought we could grab something to eat at the café and then stop by the corner store on our way back to pick up some groceries to make meals here rather than going out for meals."

Bree shut her laptop down, gathered her notes into a pile on top of it, and answered Maggie, "I didn't realize how hungry I was! The café sounds fine."

PRIMROSE Pastries, the café in the center of Gaffney where cross streets met, was still bustling when Maggie and Bree entered despite lunchtime being nearly over, with five of its six tables occupied. Each table held a small vase of flowers next to a wicker basket containing condiments, each basket was adorned with a green and white checkered ribbon that matched the green and white patterned valances at the front window and the window next to the checkout counter. The glass case next to the counter displayed an array of baked goods; behind the counter a chalk board listed various coffees and teas and daily soup and sandwich specials.

Maggie ordered soup and sandwiches for them both while Bree claimed the empty table by the window that looked out on the town center.

"I like the photos they've hung around here," Bree commented when Maggie joined her, pointing to four photos of Irish countryside scenes, each framed with wood that matched the tables and chairs. "I should add that to the suggestions I'm listing for the castle. They should showcase photos of the grounds and exterior, or maybe some of the nearby places of interest."

"How is your research coming along? When are you meeting with Jax?"

"He said he'd call this afternoon or tomorrow. I think I have enough ideas collected for an initial meeting; he can decide after that how he wants to approach things. How did your phone calls all go?"

"Coming along. I need to sort out which projects are most important, and how to stretch out my money. Next, I need to research what kind of permits or approvals I need to open a bookstore, and where to start with that."

At the table next to them, the ears on the man behind a newspaper perked up.

"I did form some plans in my mind on how I would set things up," Maggie continued, "where I would place shelves, and how to best arrange chairs and a table. I think I'd keep the walls a traditional whitewash paint, maybe I could find some lace curtains like cottages have been decorated with in some of the pictures I've seen."

"Wouldn't lace curtains blend in too much with the white walls? I think a splash of color at the windows might be a better contrast."

Always appreciative of her friend's decorating advice, Maggie thought out loud, "You might be right. Maybe you could help me find what would look best."

Their food arrived, set on white plates and accompanied by green and white checked napkins. Their beverages, an Irish breakfast tea for Maggie and mocha latte for Bree, were served in white china mugs.

"You should sell coffees and teas at the bookshop, and maybe a few desserts."

Maggie shook her head. "I might offer some tea and maybe small pieces of shortbread, but nothing big. I don't want to be seen as competition with the café being close by."

Jax's text arrived as they were finishing their meal. "Are you available this afternoon to meet up? Or is tomorrow morning better?"

"I can drive you over there this afternoon," Maggie suggested. "I'd like to explore the nature reserve a bit more anyway, clear my mind a little."

Bree agreed to meet Jax at four, suddenly nervous that she wasn't as prepared as she would have liked, hoping her ideas would fit the castle owners' tastes.

AFTER Bree and Maggie left, the man at the table behind them set his newspaper down and stepped up to the checkout counter. "Gayle, those two women who just left, do you know who they are?"

Gayle shrugged. "I've seen them here before but no, Patrick, I've no clue who they are. Should I know them?"

"The taller one with the brown hair, she's the new owner of the cottage that should have been mine!"

Gayle checked her inward sigh, careful not to let any attitude leak out, reminding herself Patrick was one of her most loyal customers and it wouldn't be beneficial for her to offer him too large a piece of her mind. "So, she's the one. She seems nice."

"Nice?" Patrick exploded, his voice so loud the café's remaining patrons all looked up to see what the commotion was about.

"Shhh! I'll thank you to keep your voice down!"

"You won't think she's nice after I tell you what I just overheard!"

"I don't think you should be listening in and repeating other people's conversations," Gayle warned.

"Then you don't want to know she's planning on opening a tea shop that will cut into your profits?"

As much as she detested Patrick's sometimes brash, offensive nature, he'd caught her attention. "Alright, go on."

"She's planning on opening a bookstore that will also offer teas and pastries. She's only a stone's throw from here. Don't you think some of your customers will be drawn away to her?"

Gayle tried to make light of the threat. "If she's not offering proper meals, I don't think it could do too much damage. There's enough business around for the both of us." Inside, though, a ripple of fear swept through her. She'd spent the past four years and most of her savings building her business up to the profitable level it was at now. Even a small tea shop might be enough to set her back.

Still, she didn't want to encourage Patrick, who had been known to not let go of an issue once his anger had been stirred. "I think we should just let her be. A bookstore would be a welcome addition to our area. If she sells better tea than I do, I might just have to up my game a bit to retain my customers. A little healthy competition might be good for us all."

Chapter Eight

Bree arrived at Allynwood Castle fifteen minutes before she was scheduled to meet with Jax. She studied the castle's front façade, then followed the sidewalk around to the back, watching how the various shrubs and trees swayed in the afternoon's slight breeze, trying to picture how the lawn and gardens would look in a few years, once Jax had restored them.

Then she entered the castle through its main entranceway, climbing the steps, noticing once again the entranceway's décor, stopping just before the reception area. She closed her eyes and allowed the feel of the castle and grounds to seep into her, soaking in its vibe, its atmosphere, what she could imagine had once been its grandeur.

Jax stepped over to where Bree stood, surprising her. "What did you think of our castle grounds?"

"Did you see me walking around outside?"

"I did." Jax didn't admit that he was intrigued, wondering what had been going through the American woman's mind as he watched her.

Bree felt a sudden rush of panic. "I hope it's okay that I entered the grounds even though I'm not a guest here."

"It's fine!" Jax's smile put Bree at ease. "What did you think of our grounds?"

"I was picturing how it would look once you re-establish the gardens the way you described them to me." Bree followed Jax to the sitting room in the rear of the castle's first floor, where Jax had wine and a cheese tray set up on the low table in front of the sofa. "I wanted to get another feel for Allynwood, to make sure the ideas I came up with fit."

"This sitting room has always been a comfortable gathering spot," Jax explained as Bree lowered herself onto the sofa. "I thought this would be a relaxing place to talk."

Bree surveyed the furniture, an eclectic mix of upholstered chairs that only matched the sofa through their complimentary shades of red, and the heavy red drapes, which seemed to her to be a soft velvet material. Relaxing, maybe, but Bree confirmed in her mind that the note she'd made to improve the room by lightening the drapery material and reupholstering the furniture so it coordinated better was the correct thought.

"Before I share my ideas, I have a couple of questions. I'm sorry I didn't think to ask them beforehand. First, it would help to know what the owners have in mind for the property. Do they want to retain or recapture a sense of the past? Or do they want to modernize?"

"From what I know, they'd like a blend of both aspects."

"Do they have a color palette in mind? What are their favorite colors?"

Jax considered all the colors that drew him in. Out of the entire rainbow spectrum and all the varied shades in between, he most loved the earth tones, colors that mirrored Allynwood's vast grounds, the trees and shrubbery that outlined its property edges, the various colors Allynwood's blooming gardens offered throughout the growing season. "Earth tones," he told Bree, once again pretending the owners were others and not himself. "They are quite partial to nature and would like to reflect that in the castle's interior."

Satisfied, Bree took a sip of wine while gathering her ideas. "Okay, to start with I'd use soft greens, tans, maybe a bit of navy blue downstairs. I'd keep each of the reception area, the dining room, and the seating area here in the same color themes, not tan, that's been overdone, but maybe soft greens with enough variations to keep them each unique.

"Your entry stairway and the stairway to the upper floors I'd paint in a cream color. The entryway has what, a half dozen mounted wildlife heads?

Trophies from hunting I'm guessing. Are they necessary?" Jax's immediate stiffening gave her the answer she needed. "Understood, they're important to the owners, but do you think they'd mind if those hunting artifacts were moved to their private residence? I think I read somewhere they live in a lodge on an off-limit edge of the grounds?"

"They do," Jax lied, telling himself that having already started down the path of deceit, he needed to continue that way. "Past owners of the castle have always been renowned for their hunting prowess; the trophy heads have held quite a bit of significance here."

Bree explained her stand, "I just think they might be a little off-putting to some guests, especially in an age when hunting is not always looked on favorably and animal treatment is an important consideration."

"Understood. I'll have to get back to you on that."

"Both stairways are painted grey. Cream would lighten them up, and for the stairway by the reception area, cream would make that amazing stained-glass window really stand out."

"What would you do with the upstairs?"

"I'd continue with nature themes, but you could pick up on some floral colors or patterns. Not too floral, of course! You don't want to scare your male patrons away! But maybe a soft rose color, a light grey like the stones outside, coral, yellow, moss green. Try to tie in some colors from the gardens where you can. The owners could decide those colors as well."

Bree set her notebook aside. She'd already given Jax quite a lot to think about; a wine and cheese break would give him space before she launched into her next topic.

Jax liked most of what she'd presented. He agreed that a lighter color palate on the walls would brighten the atmosphere inside. While he hesitated over some of her ideas, such as removing the mounted trophies along the entryway, most of her ideas were spot on.

"Have you given any thought to how you want to improve marketing of the castle?" Bree asked after a short break.

Jax felt himself tense up inside, as she brought up one of the hardest sticking points he faced. "Marketing is not one of my strengths. To be honest, I hate the word!"

"I get it!" Seeing the angst on Jax's face, Bree stifled a laugh. "It does need to be addressed, though."

"I know. Do you have any thoughts on that?"

"I know what I don't want to see."

"And that is?"

"Please, don't make Allynwood Castle a wedding destination! In my research online, I came across five or six wedding destination castles; they all look too much alike. Plus, I think if you limit yourself to the wedding destination market, you leave out a number of guests who might want an authentic Irish castle experience, who might not be able to get that here if the facilities are all booked up for wedding parties."

"That's just what I've thought!" Jax agreed. "Still, we need to come up with plans that will make this a place that would draw people in."

"There are many other ways to pull guests in. For one thing, if the owners have retained any artifacts from the history of the castle they could be displayed, and you could offer presentations on local history. Host artistic afternoons, such as drawing or painting classes, or even writing seminars. Maybe you could hold occasional craft fairs or showcase local talent, music sessions, anything like that. I saw sheep grazing as I entered the castle grounds, do the sheep belong here?"

Jax shook his head. "They're not ours, they belong to the farmer next door; we just allow them to graze here."

"You might work out with the farmer an opportunity for guests to learn something about the sheep industry, something they can't readily get elsewhere. Also, you could perhaps host occasional mystery dinners or weekends."

Jax couldn't keep up with all the ideas Bree presented! "Wow! All your ideas are excellent. You truly understand what we're trying to accomplish. I wonder, could we hire you to implement your suggestions?"

Stunned, Bree didn't know how to answer at first. Even though she knew her visit here would not be long term, she and Maggie hadn't even started to think about return flights. Now Maggie was keeping the cottage, maybe even moving here; but Bree still had a life back home and would have to return there before Riley and Regan came home for the summer. How long would a castle renovation take, she wondered. Certainly longer than the few weeks she had left before she had to return home.

"I only have a few weeks left here," Bree told Jax. "I'm sure there are local interior designers who would be better suited for the job."

"Right. I should have realized. Of course you can't stay here forever, you no doubt have a husband and family to get home to."

When Bree answered, "No husband, but a college age son and daughter," Jax breathed an inward sigh of relief, although he couldn't explain to himself why. Or didn't want to admit to himself what he felt inside. Bree intrigued him; not just her understanding of what it would take to improve Allynwood Castle, but Bree herself, the shine in her eyes, the light peach color of her cheeks.

He recalled the last time a woman had so attracted him. Kathleen, with long blonde hair and the figure of a cover model. She'd taken him in with her looks, her charm, her light, breezy laugh, and with her incredible sex appeal. For seven months he and Kathleen had dated, dining at various nearby restaurants, exploring the countryside, or enjoying drinks and quiet reflections along Allynwood's grounds.

His relationship with Kathleen had felt so easy, so natural, that with each passing week Jax was more and more certain he would build his future around her.

One evening as they watched the sun slide behind the horizon and stars start to emerge Kathleen suggested, "Kevin and Karen are going to Belize next month. We should join them."

When Jax told her he couldn't, she pressed to find out why. "I have too much to do around here," he explained.

"You have a staff to manage the castle, don't you?" Kathleen persisted. "Let them take care of the place. You haven't been on holiday for how long now?" Running her hand along the side of his face, she teased, "Don't you want to go away with me?"

Mustering all the self composure he could, Jax pulled her hand away and confessed, "I can't afford to go away right now."

Puzzled, Kathleen waved a hand around all their surroundings. "What are you talking about? You own a castle! You've got more money than Kevin, Karen and I combined!"

Jax shook his head. "When I inherited this place, I also inherited all its debt. I have a minimal staff and handle most of the work myself. There are no deep pockets here. I'm lucky to be able to manage the monthly expenses."

The only hint Jax had of a change in Kathleen's demeanor was an almost imperceptible dulling of the light in her eyes, and a slight sense of pretense behind the smile she continued to wear. They spent the rest of the evening talking about an upcoming concert in Belfast they both planned on attending.

Jax never heard from Kathleen again.

For that reason, he'd held his heart in check, had not allowed himself to become too close with any woman. Now, with Bree, he could feel the first layer of the wall he'd built up inside start to crumble. As much as he hated deceit, he knew he had to continue to keep his true status secret. If he could not persuade Bree to stay on longer, there would be no harm done.

Still, he hoped he could entice her to stay on. "There are other decorators, yes, but you have a vision for what would work here. You should be the one following that vision through to the end. If we hired you, would that convince you to extend your stay?"

Bree felt her heart race. Stay on? Help decorate the interior of this beautiful castle? She'd jump at the chance! Still, she had Regan and Riley to consider; even though they would be back at college in a few days, they had told her in no uncertain terms they weren't happy that she'd gone so far away. She would need to return home within a few weeks, before their current semesters were over. "Is it okay if I think on it overnight? There's a lot to consider."

"Of course."

As he watched Bree walk back up the driveway where she would meet

Maggie, Jax prayed she would give him a positive response. He couldn't, no, he didn't want to, see himself working with anyone else.

"How did Jax like your suggestions?" Maggie asked as Bree slid into the car after her meeting.

"He loved them so much he wants to hire me to implement them!"

"I hope you said yes! That's a fantastic opportunity! You can stay at the cottage with me, and we can share the rental car."

"I told him I have to think on it." Bree turned her eyes from the view of the soft hills surrounding them to her friend. "Maggie, I need to get home! I can't stay too much longer. Regan and Riley will be done with their school year soon. They're already mad at me for not being home during their break."

"They've each still got a month of college. You've got time to at least get Jax started with the renovations you've drawn up."

Bree knew Maggie was right. Her son and daughter would not need her for a few more weeks, she could at least start Jax out on the selection of fabrics and paints, help him work out a schedule for the projects to be done. For all that she wanted to work with interior design, Bree had had few chances to put her passion to practical use. To work on something as large scale and grand as a castle would be a golden opportunity to not only follow her love for design, it might also earn her enough experience and praise that she could find some kind of job in that field when she returned home.

"You're right," Bree told Maggie as Allynwood Castle faded away in their rearview mirror.

What she didn't say was that working with Jax would give her time to get to know him. Bree was intrigued by the bartender-handyman who had enlisted her ideas. Some spark had been ignited in her, some attraction that made her want to be around him more, find out more about who he was.

Bree had not felt this way about any man since her divorce from Carter. His betrayal of her, his affair with and marriage to Lyla had wounded Bree so deeply she hadn't even wanted to think about meeting anyone else. That part of her life was over; her sole focus now was on maintaining support for

Regan and Riley, managing to hang onto the house they had been raised in, seeing them through college and beyond.

Something about Jax drew her in, though. Maybe it was his smile, not too wide and slightly crooked, or the depth of his eyes, as if they saw deep into space and time, not just what lay on the surface. There was something behind those eyes, a history, a story; Bree wasn't sure what it was, but working with him would give her time to find out.

Chapter Nine

Patrick parked his car alongside the road two blocks away from Maggie's cottage. The cottage their ancestors had built. The cottage he thought would be his. No, should be his! Damn it! No matter what Sean McCabe had said, he was wrong.

The plans he had dreamed up for that cottage rose again in his mind. The bed and breakfast he'd designed. The income it could have generated. The chance to get back on his feet after so many of his ventures had failed.

He took a drag of his cigarette, inhaled deep, then released the smoke in one long, slow exhale, thinking as he watched the thin smoke trail drift upward and evaporate that was just how his dreams had gone. Vanished into thin air. No trace of them left to redeem.

Just once in his life Patrick would like to see something, anything, go his way.

He watched as Maggie and another woman, the same woman he'd seen her with at the café, emerged from the cottage, exchanged a few words, then stepped into a car and drove away. Just the sight of Maggie caused anger to rise within him like an earthquake rumbling underground, preparing to explode.

Like a water wheel that starts to spin when water fills each bucket, as anger filled Patrick's heart the wheels inside his mind started turning.

Maggie may have won the legal battle, but that didn't mean she would keep his cottage. He'd find a way to force her to change her mind. His warning to Gayle the day before had been just the start of his plans. He would turn business owners against her; hell, he'd turn all of Gaffney against her if that's what it took. He would make it so uncomfortable for Maggie to stay here that she'd let go of the cottage and return home, he would be next in line for it, then his plans would all fall into place. Maybe, just maybe, if he could turn this cottage into a successful business venture, he could convince Peg that he had in fact changed his ways, turned his life around, and deserved a second chance.

A damp, musty odor greeted Jax as he entered the storage room in the castle's basement. Aside from the brief tour he'd given Bree, he hadn't been in this part of the castle in several years and made a mental note now that he should inspect the foundation and walls in this underground level for any needed repairs. For now, though, he was on a mission: comb through the pieces tucked away here to see what might be worth displaying in renovated rooms, and while he was at it catalog all the contents of the room for future reference.

Over the years, objects had been added to the storage space with no regard to order. Jax worked now to organize chairs and furniture in one corner; clothing, tapestries and other textiles in another; china, kitchen pots and utensils, flower vases, and old lamps in a third corner; and outdoor tools, decorations, and the like in the fourth corner. In the center of the room, Jax placed photos, framed portraits, boxes of letters and paperwork, and books, anything of a personal nature that might reference his family's history.

This stack is what Jax focused on first. As he reviewed the framed portraits and family photos, deciding which might be worth displaying in the castle proper, he thought not just of his ancestral line, but also of the recent events that had left him sole owner of the castle and grounds.

His grandfather, Henry Doyle, had left the property to Jackson's uncle, Stephen. When Stephen succumbed to an early, incurable cancer, Jax's parents assumed ownership. Jax had thought he'd have a good number of years to help them with updates and repairs, and to marry and start a family of his own before the castle passed to him. An avalanche while his parents were skiing in the Alps ended that.

Life can turn around as fast as a branch snaps off its mother tree in a heavy wind, as quick as a saucer slips out of a hand and shatters on a hard floor. In an instant, Jax was bowed low by grief and burdened with a castle whose debts ran higher than its income.

He could have walked away from Allynwood. He could have sold it a dozen times over to developers who wanted to turn it into a luxury hotel. He could have been rich, which would have impressed Kathleen when she came along, even if a castle was not part of the holdings.

Family roots ran deep within him, though, and Allynwood was as much a part of him as the stones were a part of its walls, as if the castle's very stones were a part of his flesh and blood, cells and bones.

Memories from recent years swept through Jax's mind like the waves of the Atlantic, swishing back and forth, depositing images, leaving in their wake a flood of feelings. He thought he'd moved past the pain of his parents' loss but now, seeing their faces in so many photos from years gone by, he felt his chest tighten and his heart ache all over again. He set the photos aside, closed the door to the now semi-organized storage room, and retreated upstairs to focus on any other project that would not be so emotionally draining.

"CALL me, Mom!"

Bree reread Riley's text three times. "I don't know what to make of it," she admitted to Maggie as they returned to the cottage after a trip into Lurgan scouting out home furnishings, hardware, and specialty shops, looking for items that would fit what the castle and the cottage could use. "She never asks me to call her. I wonder what's up?"

"Only one way to find out," Maggie answered back. "Call her!" She then carried the few purchases she'd made into her bedroom, not so much because they needed storing away, but so Bree could place her call in privacy.

Bree knew she was five hours ahead of Riley, which would make it ten-thirty in the morning back home. Hoping Riley would be free, and not in a class, Bree placed the call.

"I got your text. Are you okay? What's going on?"

"I'm fine. When are you coming home?"

"Maybe not for a few more weeks," Bree told her. "I've been commissioned to help with an interior decorating project."

"Seriously? You're abandoning us for a job you could just as easily get back here at home?"

Bree recognized Riley's sarcastic tone; she'd heard it so many times before. Forcing herself to not respond to her daughter's mood, Bree told her, "It's a unique opportunity. But you didn't call to hear about that. What's up?"

"I just don't like you being so far away. I need you here."

"You haven't needed me for the past three years, ever since you were a senior in high school."

"I had to learn to stand on my own!" Riley's tone now was harsh, biting. "Ever since you pushed Dad away!"

"You mean ever since your father left us, ever since he had an affair, a very public one with his office assistant, got her pregnant and had to marry her." Bree matched Riley's harshness word for word. "I didn't push him away; he chose to leave us."

Even now, three years on, replaying Carter's words in her mind as he announced he was in love with someone else and was leaving her still shattered Bree's heart like the time a stone had hit her car's windshield at just the right angle and the window broke in a thousand pieces around her. Not that he'd had to confess to her; she'd heard rumors from a number of friends, and felt the pitying stares throughout the community they lived in every time she stepped out for lunch or coffee or walked into a shop. Whispers, rumors, stares, she'd had her fill of them to the point that, when Carter finally came clean to her, in some ways it was almost a relief.

Turning her attention back to Riley, Bree asked, "Is there something specific you need me for? Are you in trouble? Having a problem? Even though I'm not right there you can always talk to me."

Riley didn't know how to answer at first. This was so unlike her mother. The mother she knew dropped everything when her son or daughter wanted her. Her mother, after hearing Regan or Riley needed her, would spare no time or expense in rushing to their side. Her mother would certainly not be thousands of miles away, with an ocean between her and her children, for weeks at a time!

Caught off guard, unused to her mother flexing her independence, Riley could only answer, "Everything's fine Mom, I just wondered when you'd be home."

Bree remained seated in Maggie's kitchen several minutes after the call had ended. As a mother, she wondered once again if she was right to stay away for so long, even though she had nothing pressing to call her back home. As a woman with newfound independence, whether or not by choice, this opportunity to discover a new world, and new parts of herself, was too exciting to pass up. That choice came at a cost, though. Bree had never before felt she was not giving everything in her to her children. She would have to find a way to balance the guilt that came with independence.

JAX greeted Bree in the dining room, where he had fresh coffee and scones waiting. "After you left yesterday, I searched through our storage room for artifacts you might want to use once our renovations are done. I found some portraits and photos that might be good to hang on walls, and a few vases and pieces of furniture. I don't have a good eye for decorating, though. You should look at them and be the judge of what's appropriate."

"That's wonderful. I'd love to see what you found when we're ready. Right now, the owners will want to focus on painting and repairs." Bree opened her laptop and turned it at an angle so they could both see the notes and samples she had compiled. "To start with, I've gathered some paint colors and textile ideas based on our earlier conversation. I wasn't able to work out any cost estimates as I don't know reliable sources here. What I present are basic ideas; the owners can always find alternatives to what I'm showing you. These are just suggestions."

Bree opened photo after photo of mock interiors she had designed using an interior design application. "For the reception area, I think a light mint green would work. It ties in with the stone floors, the marble around the fireplace, and the wood accents. The furniture here could be re-covered with coordinating green and cream, green and light brown, or green and light grey variations; here's a green foliage pattern with cream background I think would look nice; the pattern also has olive green and flecks of wine that will coordinate with what I've selected for the dining room.

"I've already mentioned cream would look good along the stairway. Here's a sample of what it would look like.

"In the dining room, I'd use a rich, darker green. The oak tables and chairs you have there could use some polishing to make them shine, other than that they're fine although you might consider recovering the chair seats. I found this tapestry material that would make lovely drapes. The hint of mint green and the wine-colored small flowers on the fabric tie in with the reception area, lending to a coordinated flow. Here's what the room would look like with pine color walls and tapestry drapes, and I've located a fabric with cream background and thin gold stripe for seat covers if you want to try that."

Jax contrasted the old dining room, reception area and stairway with what Bree showed him now. "That's quite a difference. I wouldn't have believed how much fresh paint and a few inexpensive changes could improve a room. This is brilliant!"

"Thank you." Bree felt a sense of accomplishment she hadn't felt in years. She couldn't remember the last time Carter had complimented her on anything she'd done. Nor could she think of a recent time Regan or Riley had appreciated any of the ways she'd extended herself for them, not just the usual cooking and cleaning, but all the times she'd run out to purchase something they needed last minute, or the open door/open food policy she allowed them to offer their friends. Yes, it was part of a mother's job, and part of her job as a wife while she was married to take care of the house, the meals, and their children. Still, it would have been nice, especially in the last few years, to receive a word of appreciation from any one of them.

Feeling that she could do something well aside from house care and tending to her son and daughter's needs gave Bree the first sense of confidence, since her divorce, that she could indeed build a new life.

"I hope the owners like my ideas as much as you do." Bree turned back to her laptop. "Now, the casual sitting room I think would look good in slate blue. I've located a lighter chintz floral fabric for drapes there with mint green, olive green and wine accents as well as coral, yellow, and pink that bring the colors of your gardens, when they're blooming, indoors, and the mint, olive and wine colors coordinate with the reception area and dining room. See how the whole downstairs flows now? For the furniture upholstery, I'd keep the colors simple, light grey to complement the room's stone floors. I've chosen a light grey tweed mix for the sofa and chairs, you'll see the fabric has hints of blue and berry colors that coordinate with the walls and curtains, without contrasting patterns. You don't want the patterns in your rooms to fight with each other. I would add slate blue, mint, and berry colored throw pillows for accent pieces."

Jax listened as Bree continued to outline colors and fabrics for the upstairs bedrooms, caught up as much in her designs as in the texture of her voice, light, almost musical, and in the way her golden hair and green eyes shimmered underneath the ceiling light fixtures that adorned the room. For the first time in many months he felt two things: hope that he could in fact turn this castle around so it would compete with the more famous accommodations tourists were drawn to, and a desire to try his hand at dating once again.

"Where's the best place for me to buy some paint and a few hardware supplies?"

From a nearby aisle where he had been shopping for cheese and lunch meats, Patrick overheard Maggie ask Rita, the clerk behind the counter at Market on Main, Gaffney's smallish corner market, and turned his ear to hear the full conversation.

"You'll best find them in Lurgan, Miss. We've a few basics here, but we don't carry paints or any large hardware."

"Thank you."

Patrick waited until Maggie had left the store, then hurried up to the counter. "What did the American want?"

"Paints." Rita gave the briefest of answers; over the years she'd seen enough of Patrick's busybody, meddling ways and guarded against them now. "And what is that to you?"

"You know she's after taking over my cottage."

"The way I heard it, the cottage is hers."

"You heard wrong," Patrick lied. "The matter's not been settled yet. And what do we want with an American taking over one of our places? Shouldn't this area be left to those of us who have lived here all these years?"

Old enough and wise enough to be able to see through the lie, Rita shook her head. "Patrick, you know the matter's settled, the cottage is hers, and the sooner you give up your notions and accept Maggie as part of our town now, the better off you'll be." She turned to her stock checklist then, ending further conversation.

Undaunted, Patrick continued with his mission to smear Maggie's name.

Marian Michaels ran a bed and breakfast ten minutes away, set back from the main highway that brought tourists to the region. Patrick brought her four of her favorite currant scones and a box of tea.

"I hope you're doing well, Marian," he greeted her. "How is your business going?"

Marian sat across from Patrick in the sitting room where guests could relax and watch television. "We're off to a bit of a slow start, but it's early in the season. I've a fair stream of bookings in the months ahead; I think I'll be okay."

"Did you know there's a new lass in our town who's applying for a bed and breakfast license? Her location, right along the main road and very convenient for tourists, is sure to cut into your business. Are you going to stand for that?"

Surprised, Marian's heart sank. "First I've heard of this. I'm not sure I can stop her."

"I doubt you can get anywhere with the licensing board, but you might win by convincing people in our area that she's not welcome here."

"I don't know, that seems a bit harsh don't you think?"

Patrick shrugged. "It's your call, and your business at stake. Do what you think best."

Meeting with Conor in The Crooked Wall, Gaffney's only pub, Patrick fanned the flames harder. "What do we need with a stranger from America coming in and taking over our town?"

"Sure, she wouldn't do that." Conor sent a quizzical look back to Patrick. "I've only seen her the once, picking up a few supplies at the market she was, she seemed that nice."

"She wears that niceness like a veil, covering up what's below her sweet surface. Trust me, she's got designs on our town, wants to turn it into some tourist trap, all souvenir shops and postcard image fakery. She'll strip away all of what makes Gaffney 'ours' and turn it into some Hollywood falseness. Is that what we all want?"

Not realizing others in the pub had turned their attention to what he was saying, Patrick jumped at the outcry around him. He listened to the buzz that filled the pub, vows of "no way", and "she'll not take over our town". Leaning back in his chair with an interior smug smile, he thought, "This went better than I hoped!"

Chapter Ten

Within two weeks of finalizing her inheritance of the McCarey cottage, as she was growing accustomed to hearing it called, Maggie had given the floors a deep cleaning, had painted the front door and window trim a fresh sea blue, and had replaced the window panes that had been cracked. The roofing contractor she'd located with Sean McCabe's help had laid down sheets of vinyl on the roof's exterior to protect the interior from leaks until he could address the necessary repairs. The bedrooms had been cleaned and fitted out with fresh bed linens, one bedroom for Bree, and one for herself, and the bathroom refreshed with new towels, a small vase of silk flowers, and fresh lavender soap.

She and Bree completed their stay at the bed and breakfast and settled into the cottage. Each morning after Maggie woke, she lay in bed several minutes soaking in the cottage's peacefulness, trying to imagine the presence of her father, her ancestors. She'd read enough of the papers Liam had given her to have a basic knowledge of her ancestors' blood lines and how the cottage had passed from one person to another, although she hadn't memorized the information and still needed to check the papers at times. The few minutes of stillness each morning gave Maggie a sense of connectedness to the generations before her who had fashioned and cared for the cottage.

In between painting and sprucing up her new home, Maggie delved into the links Liam had provided, getting to know some of the history of the area she now found herself in.

Records noted a small gathering of settlers as early as the 16th century, drawn together by nearby streams which provided fish for food, and well traveled roadways that proved useful for trading opportunities and to learn of news of the world beyond their settlement.

In the 17th century the small gathering of people swelled to about eighty; a new landowner had purchased large sections of land, and the people gathered at that settlement were employed as field hands or other laborers. Cottages and markets sprang up, and by the end of the century the settlement became incorporated into a town named Gaffney.

Gaffney's population swelled in the late 1800s as the linen industry doubled and tripled in size. Fields of flax blossomed and then were harvested; and turning flax into linen, which had started as a cottage industry, became a much larger, lucrative business. Cottages rose around Gaffney as landowners rented fields and cottages to additional laborers.

The linen industry became mechanized, then in time declined as cheaper linen was processed outside of Northern Ireland. In time, cottages who had been abandoned or never fortified crumbled and returned to the landscape. Only a few of the old cottages still stood. The McCarey cottage was one.

Gaffney itself shrank back to an average population of 340 where it remained.

As Maggie went back and forth between her cottage and Gaffney she studied the town more closely, trying to visualize what the original settlement would have looked like, how it had changed over time, and where her ancestors might have walked.

In order to get to know the people of Gaffney better, Maggie stopped by almost daily at the café and the corner market, observing how Gayle and Rita each conversed with patrons who were a regular part of their days.

She wondered if her bookstore would ever develop a devoted following, if she would ever get to know the people of Gaffney as intimately as Gayle and Rita knew their customers.

While Bree spent mornings continuing research on materials for Allynwood's renovations, and afternoons helping Jax out, Maggie drew up plans for the bookstore she wanted to open, setting down a diagram of the cottage's main room and marking where bookshelves would go, and how she would arrange the small table and chairs. She measured for bookshelves and noted a few stores in Lurgan where she might find them. Maggie started a list of titles she would like to carry and where she could obtain them, and a list of local authors whose works she might be able to feature in time.

"First things first," she reminded herself one day as she rose from the kitchen table. "I'd better see Sean about the process to open my bookstore."

"It's a fairly straightforward process for what you want," Sean informed her later that afternoon. "You need to decide whether you're opening it as a sole endeavor, or a partnership with anyone else. I'm guessing sole endeavor. You'll need to choose a name for your business and choose how you're going to handle bookkeeping. There are several online bookkeeping programs to consider, unless you prefer the old hard copy method. In either case, you must be diligent about it and faithful in recording every transaction, income taken and expenses paid out. You'll need to complete tax forms on a regular basis. Once you have the basics sorted out for yourself, come see me again; I can direct you to a website to register your company, unless you want to register in person in Belfast."

"Sean, this was very helpful. Thank you. What do I owe you for today?"

With a shake of his head and a wave of his hand, Sean replied, "Nothing. Maybe a free book and cuppa once your place is opened."

"That's a deal!"

No matter how sure she was that opening the bookstore of her dreams was what she wanted, stepping out into fresh air after meeting with Sean, Maggie found her nerves heightened and her head swimming with all the decisions she had to make. Sole enterprise, that was an easy decision, a given. Tax reporting, that would be no problem once she figured out a bookkeeping system. Bookkeeping, that would take some thinking on. Maggie considered herself fairly well disciplined, and was sure she could manage faithfully tracking every sale and every expense, but she'd have to research the best methods.

Naming the business. That was the sticking point! She had only dreamed of standing in her own bookshop, chatting with customers who came in to browse her offerings, or providing tea and a treat while two or more customers sat and talked about what they'd read or wanted to read.

She had never thought of what she'd call her place. She would need a little time to find the right business name.

After days of rain, the sun shining down on Allynwood Castle's patio and gardens was too much to resist. Jax suggested to Bree, "Let's take our tea outside."

Carrying the tray that held their tea and biscuits, Bree followed him to the wrought iron table and chairs she had seen before, where the sun now shone brightest. Surveying the peonies and emerging spring flowers showing off their brightest colors in the sun's golden light, and the lush green of lawn and trees stretched out far beyond where they sat, Bree allowed a sense of calm and peace to settle inside her which she hadn't felt since her communication with Riley. Riley had not responded to the several texts and phone calls Bree had tried. When Bree asked Regan if he knew if Riley was okay, he'd only told her "I guess so, she never tells me anything!" For the past few days, she had not been able to quell her increasing sense of guilt over being away from home for so long and in effect abandoning Riley and Regan.

"If I had this view every day I'd never get anything accomplished," she admitted to Jax. "I don't know how the owners can stand to spend a minute away from this beauty."

Jax felt no sense of peace. Inside, he was torn between choosing to hold his ties to the castle and grounds close, and admitting he, in fact, owned this glorious castle and sprawling grounds. He had no real expectation of building a relationship with Bree; at some point she would return home and he would remain here, fighting to keep his castle home viable and out of the hands of corporate structures who only saw it as a money-making endeavor. Still, the scent of Bree's perfume filled the air around him even when she'd left for the day, and the light in her eyes shone through his occasional dark nights.

Seated beside her now on the patio with the world he owned displayed everywhere he looked, he could only respond, "The owners are more dedicated than you can imagine to preserving and improving their holdings, which is why your help through the renovation process is so very much appreciated."

They reviewed the plans Bree had developed, which by now had been transferred to Jax's laptop, selecting which paint samples were closest to Bree's color suggestions, pricing out textile options that might fall more within the budget Jax was doing his best to stay under, and drafting a spreadsheet itemizing tasks, color and textile options, pricing, and the order in which work should be done.

Jax's mind was not focused on work, though. Bree filled his thoughts so completely that at last he pushed his laptop aside, sat back, and suggested, "Let's take a break. The grounds are calling for us to spend some time walking among their greenery."

Uncharacteristically tongue tied, he and Bree were a third of the way down the lawn before Jax was able to ask what had been on his mind all day. "Tell me a little about yourself."

"Let's see, I live in Ohio, I'm divorced, I have a son and daughter in college, and I'm visiting here with my friend Maggie. But you already know that last part."

"What was the divorce about?" As soon as his words were out, Jax knew he'd overstepped. "I'm sorry, I shouldn't have asked. It's none of my business."

Bree shook her head. "No, it's okay. My husband, I mean my ex, had an affair with someone he worked with. She got pregnant, he divorced me and married her."

"He's a fool."

Bree almost laughed at Jax's comment. "I think so too! Now, what about you? Tell me a bit about yourself, aside from the fact that you renovate castles."

"I live nearby." Jax hoped she wouldn't ask for a more specific location. "I grew up around here. My parents wanted me to get an advanced education and build a big career. I'd rather live a more low-key life."

"Are your parents very disappointed?"

"They died not too long ago. I think if they look down on my life now they must be pleased. At least, I hope so."

Bree caught the slight strain in his voice, as if Jax fought to control some emotion or other. From the corner of her eye she caught his profile, the strong, straight angles of his chin and nose, the deep set to his eyes, the bit of hair that hung over his forehead. She felt her heart softening even further for him and had to remind herself to keep her heart in check. She was only here for a short while.

Still, she couldn't stop herself from joining her hand with his when Jax held his hand out as they strolled back to their table and chairs.

Nor could Jax help wishing he could lean over and kiss her. He restrained himself, though; timing was everything, and the time wasn't right.

MAGGIE first noticed something odd when she and Bree stopped into the café one day for soup and sandwiches. As they ate, Maggie felt several sets of eyes on her. Even Gayle seemed curt with her as she took Maggie's money and delivered their meal.

As Maggie and Bree walked to the corner market, Maggie was aware of whispers, pointing, and people avoiding them.

Maggie and Bree were both aware that conversation stopped as soon as they stepped inside the store. Eyes fixed on them averted as soon as Maggie turned their way. An air of tenseness filled the small shop; and those already inside were quick to finish their shopping, pay, and leave the store.

As Rita rang up their purchases, Maggie's curiosity got the better of her. "Have I done something wrong? Everyone seems to be avoiding me."

Rita liked the woman who stood before her. She found Maggie to be a lovely lass with a warm, open face, bright eyes that drew people in, and a soft smile that invited friendship. Maggie had done no wrong as far as Rita could see, and all the talk of late, instigated by Patrick Rita was sure, was getting out of hand. Rita had no idea how to throw cold water on the flames Patrick was inciting, but she at least could fill Maggie in on what was behind people's reactions to her.

"People are afraid you have designs on our town, that you're out to take it over, turn it into an Americanized tourist trap. Now, I don't believe a word of it, but tell me, is there any truth to that rumor?"

"What?" Maggie was so stunned she didn't know what to say at first. "No! Of course not! Where did people get that idea? Oh, wait," a thought occurred to Maggie, like light dawning across a darkened sky. "It's Patrick, isn't it? He's trying to turn people against me. You know I inherited a cottage he wanted. He thinks he can make it so uncomfortable for me here I'll go back home and the cottage will be his!"

Rita's slight nod was all the confirmation Maggie needed.

"I won't let him win!" Maggie vowed. "Thank you, Rita. You're a true friend. Maybe the only friend I have here."

"I couldn't let you continue not knowing what people are thinking." Rita finished ringing up Maggie and Bree's purchases, accepted their payment and then, before handing their bags over to them, slipped two chocolate bars in. "My treat. Now, go figure out your plans for addressing Patrick's charges. Mind, don't go at him head on, he can be a hard one."

Standing at Rita's counter, Maggie was sure she could take on whatever Patrick chose to throw at her and prevail. Once they stepped outside, though, her confidence waned.

"What are you going to do?" Bree asked.

Maggie shook her head. "I have no idea."

Jax could not get Bree out of his head. Hours after she'd left he could still feel her presence, hear the timbre of her voice, detect the faint aroma of her perfume. He'd shut off his desire for a relationship long enough. It was time to open closed doors once again, and risk whatever hurt might lie ahead for a chance at whatever joy the future might hold.

Part of him hoped the phone call he placed would go through to Bree's voicemail, part of him was elated to hear her voice when she answered.

"Bree, it's me, Jax." Cursing himself for allowing his nerves to rise so strong that he found himself scrambling for words, he pushed through them and went straight to the heart of his reason for calling. "I was wondering, would you like to have dinner with me tomorrow?"

Caught off guard, Bree hadn't anticipated a question like this coming her way, and from Jax above all. She delayed her answer so long, he asked at last, "Are you still there?"

"Oh, yes! Sorry. I just," Bree paused again, "I just had to check my calendar. Yes, dinner would be fine. Shall I meet you at Allynwood?"

"No, I'd like to take you someplace else. I'll pick you up, if you remind me again where you're staying."

She gave Jax the address of the cottage. After Jax had hung up, Bree turned to Maggie. "Jax has invited me for dinner tomorrow night."

"I'm not surprised." Maggie turned away from the internet pages of fabric samples she had been browsing through for downstairs curtains. "You and Jax are drawn to each other. I'm surprised it's taken him this long to ask you out."

"How do you even know that? You're not with us all the times we work together."

"I can see it all over your face and hear it in your voice whenever you tell me about your time spent with him." Maggie laughed. "We've been best friends for how long? I can read you like a book. A picture book. With large type captions!"

Even Bree had to laugh at that. "Maggie, what am I going to do? I don't want to fall in love again. Not with someone so far from home. There's no future in it."

"He's not asking you for a future! He's asking you for dinner. And ready or not, you're already in love with the man."

Maggie was right. Bree knew it, even if she didn't want to admit it to herself. More and more she found her thoughts centered on Jax long after their work sessions were over. When she told Jax about her divorce, a sense of mistrust of men that she had spent months burying rose to the surface again. She knew she couldn't let that mistrust hold her back all her life. Was she ready, now, to address the fears and hurt Carter had inflicted upon her, to start to heal from them so she could move forward and rebuild her future? Bree wasn't sure at all. She only knew, at this moment, that dinner with Jax was a good place to start.

Maggie stayed up an hour after Bree had gone to bed. She brewed a relaxing cup of tea, let the stillness of her cottage settle around her, and tried to quiet the thoughts that swirled in her mind.

She still had no name for her bookstore. She didn't even know where to start. She wrote down every idea that came to her, but none of them clicked yet, none of them stirred her heart or felt like the inspiring, magical name she hoped would draw people in.

Then there was Bree. Her friend had become so involved with the castle renovation project, she and Bree had not yet found time to see much of the region they had come to explore. Now Bree was in love, and Maggie was happy for her, but finding available time for touring even the most popular tourist attractions would be even more challenging.

And Patrick, and the people he was turning against her! That problem knocked loudest around the walls of her mind. She would have to convince the people of Gaffney she had no intentions of disrupting their town or doing any harm to any of them. She just wasn't sure how to go about it.

Her first thought was to talk once again with Sean. She rejected that idea, though. While he sided with her in the matter of ownership of the cottage, he was still also an acquaintance of Patrick's. Maggie was quite sure he wouldn't approve of Patrick's tactics now, but would he side with her over someone he'd known far longer, someone who was from the same area? She couldn't say for certain.

She could always have another chat with Rita about it, but that would place the storekeeper in the middle of the problem. Rita was too kind of a person for Maggie to want to involve her like that.

Liam came to mind. That had the most possibilities, Maggie thought. He was removed from the town's problems, did not live in Gaffney as far as she knew so would not have the same conflicts, and would most likely have an open mind about it all. He had once offered to give her a tour of the nature reserve he worked in; maybe while showing her around the place he could also give her some insights as to how to proceed with Patrick to diffuse any problems he tried to stir up.

She would give Liam a call tomorrow.

Chapter Eleven

Liam greeted Maggie with a smile and a hot cup of tea. "Weather's taken a wee turn to cold, so. You'll be wanting something to warm your bones."

"Thank you. Yes, it's colder now than it was this morning."

"The weather changes fast here, you'll find."

"That's not all that changes fast here." To answer Liam's quizzical look Maggie replied, "I said I hoped you'd be able to help me. I'm not sure how to handle something I'm dealing with; it involves the people in town, so I can't ask any of them."

Liam settled back in his chair, a position he assumed whenever he sensed a long discussion was about to begin. "I'm glad you called on me. Please go ahead."

Maggie had rehearsed while driving over to Oxford Island how she would approach the subject with Liam. Sitting here now, though, she still was unsure how to start. After testing out a few ideas, she at last started with, "I've been trying to connect with the people in town, getting to know them, build some friendships. I thought I was making good progress, but now people are shutting me out. They think I've come to Gaffney not just to open a bookstore, but to 'Americanize' the town, turn it into a tourist trap type place."

Even though he was sure he knew the answer, Liam asked, "Are you?"

"No! Of course not!" Maggie then explained, "I think I know who started the rumor although I can't prove it, at least not yet. My father's cousin was sure he'd inherit the cottage. He's most unhappy that it went to me instead."

"So, he's trying to drive a wedge between you and the townspeople, make you want to leave, sure the cottage would then be his." Liam considered Maggie's predicament several minutes, while they both finished their tea. Then he spoke.

"I don't know this cousin so I can't give you specifics on how to deal with him. Let's look at the situation in general, though.

"Many people here lead small lives. By small, I mean they don't carry many dreams inside them. They don't look beyond the stone walls that define the fields around them. They see the ocean, but don't look beyond its horizon. It's enough for them to find a steady job, earn enough to feed their families, pay their bills, keep body and soul together without spending time and energy on dreams that evaporate like the morning mist, or are blown away in a heavy sea breeze.

"I would venture a guess that this cousin of your father's was one of the few who had a dream. He wanted the cottage for more than just a home. Mind, I've no idea what his plan would have been, but your moving into the cottage thwarted his plan."

"So he'll try everything he can to make me want to leave."

Liam nodded in agreement with Maggie. "I don't know how far he'll push the matter, but I doubt he'll give up easy."

Maggie turned Liam's words over in her mind, examining them from various angles, looking for any glimpse of light shed on what to do next. When no ideas came, she asked Liam, "What do you think I should do?"

"For now, stay clear of him. Continue being friendly with the people in Gaffney, making small inroads, showing them you want to be part of their community. If anyone asks, keep reiterating that you have no plans to change their town, just to blend in with them."

He gave Maggie a moment to digest this, then asked, "Who in town would you say you've established more of a friendship with in the past few weeks? Can you think of one or two people?"

"Rita, the woman behind the market counter, seems very nice." Maggie recalled how Rita had confided in her, trusted her. "And Gayle, she runs the café in town, I thought she would be a great person to talk with about opening a business, but lately she's one of the people who have become very distant."

"You might start with either of them. If they were friendly before, they might open up to you now if you approach them in a non-threatening way."

Maggie considered his suggestion. "I suppose I could try. If they choose not to talk with me, it won't be any worse than what they're doing now."

"That's the way to approach it." Liam agreed, then continued, "I don't know if you've had a chance to look into any of the websites I recommended."

"I did, I read up on Gaffney's history, and a bit about the linen industry." Maggie thought again of the linen industry article, how it stirred a passion in her spirit she hadn't expected. "I was fascinated by the process of turning flax into linen."

"I can send you some more history on that if you'd like." Liam jotted down a note on a pad on the table in front of him. "I'm also going to add a few more links."

Looking at Maggie again, Liam explained, "I don't know how familiar you are with Irish and Northern Irish history. Northern Ireland is still tied to Britain, still part of the United Kingdom and not technically part of Eire itself. Most likely you've heard at least a little about the Troubles we had here in the North from the late 1960s to the late 1990s. Our history is at times at least as complex as your American history is.

"Gaffney was ruled by the British from the 1600's on. The breakdown of ethnicity has always been mixed, with British citizens holding a bit larger percentage. I believe there's more of a mix of Irish and British sentiments there now; but you'll notice that while you will see a British flag flying around here on occasion, you'll not likely find an Irish tricolor waving in the wind. Just as in America mistreatment of Native Americans and Negroes caused a lot of hardship and left many scars, there are many scars on both sides here in our North. You should become familiar with more of our history, but until you know the people of Gaffney better you should stick with the websites I send you, and if you have any questions discuss them with me. The caution to not discuss politics or religion is especially true here, with the added caution to not take sides or even discuss our history until you truly know who you're talking with. As a newcomer, you will do especially well not to comment on local issues. Remain as neutral and uninvolved as possible."

By the time they finished their conversation the wind had decreased, and even though steel grey clouds still clung to the sky and mirrored themselves in the lough below, Liam offered Maggie, "Would you care for a tour around our grounds? The weather's cleared a bit now."

"Yes please, that would be great."

They first looked out over the lough that surrounded the information center. "Every year we are a stopping over point for a number of waterfowl species, including grebes and mergansers, as well as other migratory birds. We have four miles of trails, and several blinds which enable photographers and other bird enthusiasts to view our winged guests up close.

"Our trails give visitors a chance to not only see birds and other wildlife, but also to discover various species of trees, shrubs, and wildflowers. Markers along the way identify some species, and there's more information in our center for anything visitors might want to ask about."

As they walked along the main lough trail, Liam informed Maggie, "Over the last several years we've been working at reviving and improving our wetlands and bog areas along the edge of the lough. These are vital areas for wildlife preservation, a critical part of our ecosystem."

Maggie studied the edge of the lough where Liam was pointing, where brown rushes, greening vegetation and standing water mixed with brown soil replaced the lough's rippled waters. With her limited knowledge of ecosystems and no information on bog life, the lough edge region looked like wasteland to her; she would have to take Liam's word for it that the wasteland was beneficial.

As they followed the path back to the center, Maggie was captivated by a pair of swans bobbing along on the water's surface, and by the call of birds she could not name, making a mental note to research more about the birds and other wildlife she might find at the reserve. Promising to return and learn more through the programs and material the reserve had to offer, Maggie thanked Liam for his time and advice.

"I wasn't at all sure who to turn to. Thank you for taking the time to listen and help me out."

"I'm honored you felt you could turn to me," Liam responded. "Please let me know how you're getting on, or if you have any further questions."

THE restaurant Jax took Bree to was a long, low thatched roof cottage that had been converted into a restaurant and pub. Bree marveled at the stained-glass windows and panels the restaurant had been adorned with, and the stenciled Celtic knotwork design that ran along the walls where they met the roof line.

"I hope you don't mind that I chose this restaurant instead of a more upscale one," Jax apologized as they waited for their glasses of wine to arrive. "The food here is outstanding, and the atmosphere a bit more authentic."

"I don't mind at all! I'd rather have authentic than overdone. Was this really someone's cottage once?"

"Yes, up until about fifteen years ago."

Bree glanced around again, taking in the dark wooden beams that supported the ceiling throughout. "Would a thatched cottage have a solid wood roof like this?"

"Most of the time now, yes. A long time ago no, the thatching would show on the inside."

Bree's eyes shone when she faced Jax again. "Thank you for bringing me here. I would have gone home without knowing how charming one of these cottages was. Just think, now I've seen a real thatched cottage, and I'm working at a castle!"

Jax, captivated by the way stars shimmered in her golden hair, or the hint of rosy sunset in her cheeks, or the way her seafoam green sweater brought out all her colors in a way that unsettled him through and through, agreed. "You're having quite the experience, aren't you!"

Bree forced herself to look at the menu before her rather than the man seated across from her. You don't know the half of it, she thought, glimpsing over the edge of her menu Jax's wine colored sweater, avoiding looking up to his broad shoulders and his freshly shaved face.

After ordering their dinners, Bree commented, "The castle upgrades are looking good. I hope the owners are as pleased as I am so far."

Jax shook his head. "No. We're not talking business tonight. We do enough of that during the day."

"Alright. Not work related, but how did you come to work at the castle? How long have you been there?"

Jax's conscience told him this was the moment he should tell Bree the truth, confess the castle was his, that he was more than just a worker there.

His fear that the truth would change Bree's view of him held him back.

"I started working there several years ago," he lied. "I live nearby, had always been fascinated by the castle, and when I heard they were looking for a handyman and groundskeeper I applied and was thrilled when they hired me."

"What happens to your job once the renovations are complete?"

"I'll always have a hand in the building and grounds there." Bree watched as Jax's face grew animated as he described his goal of restoring the gardens surrounding the castle. "I've located photos of what the gardens looked like at the height of their glory. I want to make those gardens come to life again. That will take a few more years."

"Besides the castle grounds work, what do you do? Do you have a family? What is your house like? What are your dreams?"

Jax felt himself sink deeper in a quagmire of deceit as he answered, "No family, a modest house. My dreams?" Here, at least, he was truthful. "My dream is to see Allynwood restored to the beauty it once had, to see it become a vibrant tourist destination without losing its integrity."

Jax stopped. Integrity? What a funny word to use when in the same breath he knew he was lying. He should risk making Bree angry, even having her turn away from him completely, by revealing the truth. What did it matter anyway? She was not from here. She would return home soon enough. He had no hope of a future with her.

Still, Jax could not bring himself to be honest. Instead, he diverted the conversation. "What about you? What are your dreams?"

Bree weighed her response. Part of her wanted to tell Jax her dreams all ended when Carter chose a younger woman over her, when he chose to forfeit their marriage to follow his own lusts. She had no need for dreams now. She had no desire to open the door of her heart to the hurt that came when dreams crashed to the ground.

Another part of her, though, realized one of her dreams had been reawakened, and confessed that now. "I used to dream of building an interior design business of my own. I'm not sure I'm ready to open my own business now, but our work at Allynwood might open a few doors in that field when I get home. Right now, I'm inspired watching Maggie follow her dream of opening a bookstore."

"How is Maggie's cottage coming along?" Jax wondered.

"Fine. She's cleaned the place up quite a bit, finished a few repairs and scheduled one or two more. She's ordered bookshelves for the books she wants to carry. She just needs to file her business certificate and order her stock, then she'll be ready to open."

"Will you be helping her run the bookstore?"

"You mean once the castle upgrade is done? No, I'll stay for the opening but will have to go home after that."

Jax knew he might not be able to stop her from leaving, but he could maintain a presence in her life. The best place to start was to encourage and support her dream.

"When you do go back," Jax told Bree, "when you start building your own interior design dream, I'll give you all the letters of recommendation I can. When people see how you're transforming Allynwood they'll want you to work the same magic for them!"

Long after Bree returned to Maggie's cottage, Jax's words remained with her. He hadn't laughed at her dream or ridiculed it the way Carter had each time she brought it up. Carter's lack of support over time had drained her to the point where she had abandoned her dream altogether.

Earlier that day she'd seen a curious insect in Maggie's back garden, a pale green bug with clear, gossamer wings. She marveled at how, despite its glassy, fragile appearance it flew, sailing on the afternoon breeze as if it reveled in the ride. In a similar way, now, her dream seemed as fragile and thin as that insect's wings. Perhaps, with the right support, her interior decorator dream, too, could fly.

W<small>HILE</small> driving back to town, Maggie considered how best to follow Liam's advice. She decided she would start where she first learned of the problem. Entering Rita's corner market, she browsed the shelves, picking out a package of cookies (she still had not gotten used to calling them biscuits), a box of tea bags, and a chocolate bar, all the while aware of the market's other customers who eyed her but kept their distance.

When the market had emptied of other patrons, Maggie approached the counter. "Just these, please," she told Rita. Glancing around once more to make sure they were alone, Maggie went on, "Thank you again for what you confided in me yesterday. I've been thinking over the best way to proceed."

Rita accepted the payment Maggie handed to her, then told her, "I've been considering this as well. I think you should let me talk with people, convince them what they're hearing isn't true."

"Rita, thank you, that's a very kind offer. I was thinking I'd like to reach out to a few people personally, try to develop a friendship or two. I was thinking I'd start with Gayle at the café. She's always seemed like she'd be a good friend."

Rita nodded in agreement. "Gayle has a good heart. Once she understands you have no ill intentions and you have her on your side as well as me, the rumors will stop."

Maggie found confronting Gayle more intimidating, but she could not put it off. She waited until the last of the café's afternoon customers had been waited on, then approached Gayle.

"Do you have a minute? I need to ask you something."

Several days ago, Gayle would have stepped from behind the counter if the café was not too busy and would have sat down with Maggie, glad for a chance to chat with the town's newcomer and get to know her. Now, if the rumors were true, Maggie posed a threat to her café's success. Gayle knew the only way to find out was to hear Maggie out. "Sure."

Maggie spoke quietly so the café's customers could not hear. "I understand there's a rumor going around that I intend to compete with your business and disrupt the town."

"Yes, I've heard that."

"It's not true. None of it."

"Why would anyone lie about that?"

"I wish I knew. What I can tell you is, I'm hoping to open a bookstore soon. Nothing more. My friend suggested I offer tea, maybe a few sweets as well; but I've already rejected that idea as I don't want to compete with you or take away any of your business. That's the truth. Anyone telling you anything other than that is lying."

Gayle studied the woman who stood before her. Maggie did not seem deceitful, she appeared open and honest, if Gayle was any judge of character. She'd watched Maggie and her friend a few times when they'd eaten at the café, had thought they seemed kind and would be a good fit for the community. She'd also known Patrick for ages, knew he could have a scheming side to him, hadn't wanted to believe his words about Maggie but had out of a need to protect her business. "If what you say is true, if you're not planning to compete with me or draw business away from me, swear it to me now."

A flash of impatience burned inside Maggie. How many times would she be forced to repeat her words? Shouldn't once be enough? Forcing herself to speak clearly without a trace of frustration, she once again insisted, "I swear, I have no intention of trying to draw business away from you."

"Alright, I believe you." Gayle once again sized up the woman before her. Maggie had courage, she thought, opening a new business in a country she'd never been to before. Whatever Patrick's game was, Gayle would no longer play along. She reached into the glass case displaying various pastries and desserts, pulled out two lemon tarts, wrapped them in a bag and handed them to Maggie. "Take these home for you and your friend. I'm sorry for the misunderstanding. Give me a few days to straighten out the minds of a few people who are under the wrong impression. Oh, and I don't see the harm in you offering a good cuppa with the books you sell. You have my blessing on that."

NIGHT fell soft and slow on the cottage about Maggie. In the back garden, a pair of robins called evening songs to each other, while the tree cast long shadow fingers across the grass. Inside, the candle she had lit to enhance the central room's atmosphere flickered, driven by a draft she could not see or feel.

Bree was asleep in the front bedroom, having returned home from her dinner with Jax and recapped the evening as she and Maggie sipped a bedtime glass of wine. Maggie wished she, too, would find sleep easy to come by. Too many thoughts swirled about her mind, though.

Naming her proposed bookstore proved harder than she'd imagined. She wasn't worried about any other aspect of starting the new business, filling out the forms, setting up an accounting system, investing in materials; but the name, well, that should be catchy enough to draw people in, but also, in her mind anyway, reflect a connection with the town or the cottage's history. None of the ideas that crossed her mind suited.

At least one thing had been resolved, or at least was on its way to being settled. Rita and Gayle now knew any rumors they'd heard about Maggie's intentions were lies, that she meant no harm to anyone. Over the next few days, they would correct any false impressions others in town had.

Maggie thought on Liam's advice to develop a deeper knowledge of the area, of Ireland as a whole, of their culture and customs. That seemed like a tall order to her; she wasn't quite sure where to start.

Ever since they'd arrived here, she and Bree had built a list of a number of sites they wanted to visit, ranging from scenic spots to stone circles, ancient ruins, and historic buildings. Maggie considered their list now. The destinations they'd chosen would be a good start in helping her get to know the region better. Besides, until she chose a business name she didn't feel she could proceed any further with her plans. Bree had informed her the castle renovations were well in hand, that during the next several days Jax would be focused on painting various rooms. Perhaps now would be a good time for her and Bree to step away from the projects that had kept them so busy and chip away at their sightseeing list.

Maggie turned the idea over several times in her mind, each turn casting new light as a prism in sunlight reflects new colors. Studying a map of the island, Maggie drew up an itinerary she thought would cover the best variety of sites that would fit within a week of travel. Come morning, she would go over her plan with Bree and, if Bree agreed, they would take some time off to explore the island they had unexpectedly found themselves on.

Chapter Twelve

Two days later, after fine tuning their itinerary, sorting accommodations and packing, Maggie and Bree headed out to explore the land they had come to.

Their first stop was the Clonmacnoise monastery ruins near the town of Shannonbridge. Established in the sixth century, the Clonmacnoise complex spread across meadows that ran alongside the Shannon River. Once a vital monastery whose central location drew those who wanted to study religion, increase learning, or improve their abilities in various crafts and trades, Clonmacnoise drew scholars from both Ireland and Europe. By the thirteenth century, with the rise of other churches and monasteries and the growth of the nearest village Athlone, which became a vital center for trade, Clonmacnoise was abandoned.

Bree found herself drawn to the intricate carvings worked into the high cross known as the Cross of the Scriptures, whose carved panels included the crucifixion of Jesus, the last judgment, and Christ in the tomb. She marveled over how the stones that made up various ruin wall arches had been shaped perfectly in order to fit with exact precision, and how, centuries later, those arches still stood while the buildings they were set in were eroding, worn by weather and time.

Maggie was more curious about the history of Clonmacnoise. While Bree studied stone carvings and artistic angles of the various building ruins, Maggie was intrigued by the historical notes and artifacts she found in the visitor center. As she read about the monastery's history and the many attacks Clonmacnoise had endured, she learned for the first time the stories of high kings, clan battles and elements of Irish history she'd never been exposed to before.

Bree wandered the various building ruins, taking photos as she walked. Maggie found herself drawn to one of the two round towers at the site. O'Rourke Tower, as she later learned it was called, consisted of a doorway cut through stone several feet up, a few narrow window slots and, curious to her, no capstone which should have served as the roof.

Walk the base of the tower, she heard a voice inside her whisper, and so she did, moving in a clockwise direction, and was rewarded with a sense of connection to some ancient secret she had yet to decipher.

At the entry gate to Clonmacnoise a curious statue stood, carved in black, of a man in a hooded cloak with his face buried in his left hand while his right hand rested on a staff.

"The Pilgrim," Bree commented, pointing to a plaque denoting the sculpture's name. "I would have thought a pilgrim arriving here, seeking edification, would have shown more excitement."

Consulting her phone, Maggie informed Bree, "The statue depicts a man named Aedh, son of an Irish chief, who after a long journey to Clonmacnoise was so exhausted he died upon arrival."

Bree and Maggie stood in silence before the statue, trying to comprehend how arduous a journey Aedh must have faced, what would have compelled him to travel such a long, hard road, wondering whether he'd felt any moments of relief at reaching his destination before he collapsed.

The next day they drove to the Cliffs of Moher, one of Ireland's most iconic sites. Maggie and Bree both walked towards the cliffs with anticipation of what they were about to see. While they had seen many photos of the cliffs, nothing prepared them for the dramatic landscape that greeted them.

Carved out over centuries by wind, rain and sea, the Cliffs of Moher are a series of undulating wave-like cliff edges, ranging from three hundred to seven hundred feet high. Layers of shale, sandstone and sediment stand exposed, while the Atlantic continues its ceaseless flow in and then back out. A fair breeze that day created white capped waves, while sunlight caused the Atlantic's waters to glisten like a vast field of diamonds.

Bree gazed out at the Atlantic's endless waters spread out before her, so wide no land appeared aside from the coastal cliffs she stood on. For the first time since coming to Ireland, the magnitude of the distance between herself and Regan and Riley, and the town she'd lived in all her life, overwhelmed her. Ever since coming to Ireland, she had been focused on Maggie's property and plans, and then her castle renovation plans with Jax, all of which she found exciting. Today though, with fewer distractions on her mind, Bree stood at the edge of her present world and felt the pull of her true world like waves crashing over her.

She belonged home, not here. She knew that. Her work with Jax would conclude soon enough. Her time allowance would expire. Unlike Maggie, who had access to UK citizenship through her father, who now owned Northern Ireland property and would soon have a going business concern, and would be allowed to stay in Northern Ireland as long as she chose, Bree had no valid excuse to extend her stay. What she would face back home she wasn't sure, but her time away had changed her. The big house she and Carter had bought, which she had retained as part of their divorce settlement, felt too large now. She much preferred a smaller place, cozy and inviting, where walking through empty rooms did not send echoes and memories to haunt her. She was gaining a new sense of who she was, a mother devoted to her children's needs but no longer at their beck and call, starting to flex her own independent wings. She also felt a fresh desire to delve into interior design, find a proper job where she could gain more knowledge and experience, and in time build her own clientele.

As she considered what awaited her at home, Jax entered Bree's mind. To say Jax intrigued her would be an understatement. Her heart was more and more drawn to him, to his dark brown eyes set in a thin, strong face, to that charming accent of his; but more than that, she was captivated by his passion for the castle he worked at, how he cared about every detail, even the smallest ones, of the renovation work that connected them. His agreement with her marketing ideas, rather than allowing the castle to be swallowed up by a corporate wedding destination developer thus shutting out a large segment of tourism, pleased her. He also had shown so much sincere interest in her own dreams. If she'd ever hoped to find someone she might fall in love with again, Jax fit the description.

But he was just a vacation romance, she reminded herself. Intriguing because of his appealing locale, his different culture. Bree had never entertained the idea of a vacation affair before, yet here she was heading towards one now. Jax was fascinating. He was also safe. They could both enjoy the feeling of appealing to someone of the opposite sex without the risk a serious and attainable relationship entailed. They could flirt a bit, enjoy their mutual attraction to each other, and know at the end of the day their worlds would remain the same. He lived on this side of the ocean, while her true life was on the other, and the sea between them too wide to bridge long term.

Maggie gazed out at the expanse of ocean before her, marveling at the varied shades of blue it carried, at the swirling patterns of white wave caps mixed with blue waters, at the ocean's depth and force, how it hammered away relentlessly at the rocky cliff side below her. As she studied the vastness of the waters, she began to understand how great an impact it had not just on the coastline, but on the people who had for centuries inhabited the island she now resided on. She began to understand how susceptible its inhabitants were to whatever weather the ocean threw their way, how vulnerable they were to damaging storms. She felt the isolation an island surrounded by water might have felt, and how interdependent on each other its residents would have been. Maggie had a deeper sense of why the fishing industry was such a vital part of Ireland. She could also imagine to a deeper degree the hardships past immigrants would have faced crossing the ocean in ships, no matter how big or small those vessels may have been. One would have to be desperate indeed to undertake such a dangerous journey.

Maggie studied a section of cliffs where gulls were nesting. To her the cliff ledges seemed a precarious place to try to build nests, lay eggs and raise chicks, and she wondered how many of them survived.

Dwarfed by the massive cliffs upon which she stood, and the endless panorama of the Atlantic before her, Maggie felt small and insignificant, a feeling that remained with her throughout the rest of the day.

Before checking into their accommodation for the night, they stopped by the Galway Famine Memorial. The central stone of the three stones standing paid tribute to a lighthouse and the captains and crews who carried so many Irish immigrants to distant lands. The two stones that flanked the central one were designed to look like ships' sails. Inscribed on those two stones were the names of various ships that carried starving, desperate Irish men, women and children away.

A quick internet search on her phone provided Maggie with enough background information on the famine to understand it wasn't just the potato crops that had failed, but also a systemic failure of the ruling powers to adequately provide for their people.

Maggie tried to visualize what it would be like to board a ship knowing you might not survive the journey, knowing you would most likely never again see those you were leaving behind. What would it have felt like watching that lighthouse shine out one last time, its light fading as your ship pulled farther and farther away?

What would it have felt like to remain behind, knowing hundreds around you were starving to death and you might be next?

Long after Bree had drifted off to sleep, those thoughts kept Maggie awake.

Donegal castle, their next destination, surprised both Bree and Maggie with its appearance.

"I thought it would be more regal, much larger," Bree confessed.

"I didn't expect such angular lines." Maggie pointed to the castle's boxy structure.

Bree agreed, "It doesn't have the round towers or turrets the more romantic castles all share."

"It does seem rather stark. Maybe its grandeur lies more inside." With that, Maggie led the way through the castle's entrance.

Instead of grandeur, inside Donegal Castle's walls they found a sparsely furnished, but well maintained, medieval style interior. The lower level, with a well-polished cobblestone floor, was a wide open room adorned with barrels, baskets and other storage function furnishings, and arched and narrow windows suitable for defending a castle against invaders. The stairway that would have led to upper bedroom chambers was constructed with irregular stairs, another defense tactic that would have confused and slowed invaders.

The second, main floor, opened to a banquet hall whose central feature was a polished wood table and chairs set on a woven rug. A sideboard stood against one wall, the opposite wall featured a fireplace; both the sideboard and the fireplace mantel bore finely carved details.

Bree's eyes were drawn to the bowed window at the front of the room, noting how light passing through its panes flooded the room, and to the few paintings and musical instruments that graced the room's walls. She admired the austere elegance that permeated the room, making a mental note to repeat that concept where she could with designs in the future.

While Bree studied decoration and use of light, Maggie studied the information panels placed around the room, as she had the ones on the lower level. She read how Red "Hugh" O'Donnell, one of the Irish clan chieftains, had originally built Donegal Castle, only to burn it to the ground before it fell into English hands, and how an English captain, Basil Brooke, came into possession of and rebuilt the castle.

She read about the Flight of the Earls, the last departure of Irish chiefs from Ireland, signaling the end of the old Gaelic order, giving England full rule over Ireland for centuries to come, and was surprised to find tears fill her eyes as she came to learn another layer of her ancestral land's history. If asked, she would not have been able to say why the story left her sad; she knew her heart had, over the years, been moved in ways she did not understand. She still had so much to discover about this land she had been led to.

As they slid into their car the next morning, Bree asked, "I know our next stop is Derry, but could we take a quick run up to Malin Head? It's not too far away from Derry, and I've been reading a lot about an antique store there."

"I don't see why we couldn't." Maggie handed her phone, already opened to a GPS app, to Bree. "Give me the directions as we go!"

The Curiosity Shop at Malin Head turned out to be a smallish building with an eclectic collection of treasures. Bree and Maggie browsed through the various tables and shelves, almost overwhelmed by the shop's wide selection. Maggie found a small heart shaped Irish porcelain dish with a delicate spray of shamrocks painted on its center. Bree found an antique silver ring with birds set into it, two small paintings of pastoral Irish scenes she thought might fit well on the walls of the castle, and, last minute, a leaf shaped dish with the Derry crest that intrigued her.

"You'll want to be checking out the lookout tower after this, so." The old man behind the checkout register commented as he rang up their purchases. "Mind the wind as you go; it's a bit brisk out there today."

Brisk was hardly the word, Maggie thought as she and Bree found themselves a short while later at a rugged stretch of land with a large stone tower which she learned was named Lloyd's signal tower, as it had at some point been used to signal ships offshore. From where they stood at the tower, shielding themselves from the strong winds blowing off the sea across the open stretch of land that surrounded them, they could see "80 Eire" spelled out with rocks on the shore below them. Curious as to what the sign meant, Maggie searched on her phone and discovered it was a signal to World War II pilots that they had crossed into neutral Ireland territory.

Unlike the rolling green hills and gentle scenery they'd seen in abundance as they'd driven across Ireland the past few days, Malin Head was comprised of rocky, hilly terrain, with few inhabitants spread across the rough land. Few cottages or farmhouses stood here, few sheep or cattle grazed the rock strewn landscape. Maggie wondered at the toughness of the people who made their living in this remote corner of Ireland, where hard winds blew steady and crashing waves eroded even the hardest rock over time.

From Malin Head they drove to the city of Derry. After parking their car outside the bed and breakfast place they had booked, they set out to explore the city they had been most curious about.

They toured the Guildhall, with its massive pipe organ and stunning stained-glass windows, and the Peace Bridge which stretched across the River Foyle to connect both sides of the city. Then they joined a walking tour along the top of the city walls which encircled the old portion of the city, followed by a tour of the Bogside area where much of the Troubles decades earlier took place.

"I don't know about you," Bree commented after the tour was over, "but my head's swimming from too much history, and my stomach's growling! Let's find a place for dinner."

"Agreed!" Maggie scanned the main thoroughfare they were on, spotted several possibilities, and offered them to Bree. "We could go to the restaurant on the left for a full dinner, or try the sandwich shop further down on the right for a quick meal and then check out some of the pubs in town. It's the weekend, and I'm guessing some of them will have live music."

"Let's do the sandwich and pub option!"

Nourished and refreshed, the two set out to explore Derry's night scene. Pubs, they discovered, were often small and crowded, while a few of the restaurants that offered live music were less cramped for space. After trying several places, they chose a restaurant near the town center where a trio of musicians were playing soft rock covers. They found a spot at a table a young couple had just vacated, ordered drinks and appetizers, and settled in to enjoy the music and atmosphere.

"I know it's not time yet, but I'm really going to hate to go home," Bree confessed. "I didn't plan for a long trip; I never dreamed I'd be working on a castle redecorating project!"

"You should find a job interior decorating once you go home. The Allynwood Castle project would be a great reference for you."

"If it turns out well. I'll have to return home before it's finished; I hope I can help from home when it's time."

Maggie caught the mix of sadness and disappointment that flooded Bree's eyes. She knew what troubled her friend the most. "What will you have the hardest time leaving behind? The decorating work? Or Jax?"

Bree felt her face grow hot. "Is it that obvious?"

Maggie laughed. "You know I can read your mind!"

Instead of laughing or smiling back, Bree looked even sadder. "I should never have let myself start to have feelings for him. I can't stay here forever. I need to go back home to the twins soon. Their semesters will be over and they'll be home for the summer. And Jax loves working at the castle; he would never pack his life up and move to the States! There could never be anything lasting between us."

"It's not that easy, is it?" Maggie had gone through one or two ill-fated romances of her own; she knew the pain Bree had in store. The heart isn't always practical when igniting a spark inside itself. It seldom takes stock of what would make the most sense between two people, whether they're a good fit, whether a romance has the slightest chance of working out long term. It only knows it is suddenly attracted, and a spark becomes a steady flame or, in some cases, a raging inferno. Whether the flame will remain ignited or in due course burn out, the heart itself cannot predict. It can only lead one down a path of passion, and see what fate allows.

Bree agreed, "Never easy. But I'm old enough to not let myself get carried away like some silly schoolgirl."

"From the little I've seen, I don't think it's just you." Maggie watched hope light Bree's eyes. "I think Jax is just as drawn to you as you are to him."

It's funny how the universe will send a sign at precisely the moment it will impact us the most. As Bree took in Maggie's words and allowed herself a slight bit of hope that she and Jax had something between them that might be real, an image caught the corner of her eye. She turned for a closer look; indeed, the man who had just sat down two tables away looked like Carter. In fact, he looked so much alike he could have been Carter's twin.

In that moment, all the unhappy memories of her failed marriage swept over her, all the arguments, all the wounds, the affair which had been the final straw that ended their marriage. In a flash, it all washed over her like a deluge. And in that instant, Bree wondered what she was even doing entertaining any thoughts of a new relationship. After her divorce, she'd vowed she would never fall in love again. Now here she was, not only allowing her heart to be pulled back down that path, but with someone she'd never see once she returned home.

She was a fool! Yet all while she recognized that, she wasn't at all sure she could switch off her feelings towards Jax.

Their last stop before returning to Maggie's cottage was Giant's Causeway. A fair wind blew, but the rain showers of the past couple of days had subsided, and the sun peeking in and out of puffy clouds sustained them through the breeze.

They took each other's photos standing atop the iconic stack of basalt columns near the center of the expansive rocky field and prevailed upon another tourist to take a photo of them together.

While Bree looked for various formations described in the guidebook they'd purchased: the granny, the pipe organ, the boot, Maggie was once again mesmerized by the ocean's waves, driven by the wind, rushing against the rocky shore with so much force that each wave sent huge sprays of mist rising up a good two or three feet high.

As she watched the waves roll in and out, and studied how the water washed over various basalt columns, draping the rocks in water curtains, or leaving tiny ponds on basalt column surface, Maggie reviewed all she'd learned of Irish history over the past several days, and the sceneries she'd taken in. She'd come to Northern Ireland to settle an unexpected inheritance and found a growing passion for the whole of the Irish isle. The more she saw and learned, the more she wanted to discover.

Maggie needed to finalize her ability to stay in Northern Ireland. She needed to follow through not just on her British citizenship which would allow her to stay, but also move ahead with her plans to open her bookstore. In order to open her bookstore, she had to have a name for it.

Maggie considered once again the inheritance that had brought her here. With Liam's help, she had traced the history of the cottage back to her great-great-grandfather, Nathaniel. Without him, she would never have set foot in this land. If Nathaniel had not built the cottage, and passed it down to his son, and so on, her father would not have had ownership of it, and it would not have come her way.

The line of possession was as interconnected as the basalt columns laid out before her. As she considered how deep the connections ran, both in stone and in heritage, the ideal name for her bookstore came to her.

She would call it Nathaniel's Place.

Chapter Thirteen

The day after they returned from their week of travel, while Bree had taken their rental car to check in at the castle to see what progress had been made in her absence, Maggie powered up her laptop and started filling out various forms to finalize licensing her bookstore, and to extend her stay in Northern Ireland. For the better part of two hours she typed in information, at times stopping to research what would be a proper answer, at times puzzling over how best to word a section. When a knock on her front door broke her concentration she was grateful for respite, no matter how brief, from the online application process.

Gayle stood on her doorstep, a box of baked goods in her hands. "A peace offering," she explained, holding the box out to Maggie.

Maggie stepped aside to allow Gayle entry. "I'm not sure what the peace offering is for, but come in."

Gayle accepted the kitchen chair Maggie pulled out for her. "We haven't been terribly kind to you the days before you went on holiday. That's all sorted now, you won't have any further problems from anyone in town."

"Thank you, I'm glad for that. You didn't need to bring a peace offering, though."

"We'll call it a restart, then." Gayle opened the box to reveal a half dozen currant scones. "Why don't you put your kettle on, if you've time. I'd love a tea break while my staff handles the café."

Over tea and scones, Maggie confessed, "I appreciate whatever you did to help straighten out any misunderstandings people here have had. I'll admit, the past couple of weeks I've wondered whether I was doing the right thing here."

"I know that feeling." Gayle thought back to her own dream, and how hard it was to make it come true. "My idea of opening a café almost fell apart. I was so scared, and I hit so many roadblocks along the way from glitches in financing, to unexpected problems with the building, to a slow start that made me question if I even knew what I was doing."

"Add hostility from the people where I plan to open my bookstore and you can understand my situation. You know what scares me the most? I had visions of me opening the store, lasting maybe a month, and returning home flat broke financially and emotionally."

"That won't happen," Gayle assured Maggie.

"I hope not. Would you like a peek at what I've done so far and what my plans are?"

"I'd love that!"

Maggie waved her hand around the kitchen. "My plan here, over time, is to replace the countertop and cupboards, and update the room overall." Leading Gayle to the bathroom, Maggie told her, "The same with this room, I'd like to update the faucets, maybe replace the tile. These are both projects for down the line, once I have the bookstore up and running."

Viewing both bedrooms, Gayle noted, "I like how you've coordinated the bedspread and curtains here. Both rooms have the same blues and greens, but the patterns are different."

"That was my friend Bree's idea. She thought the matching colors would tie the rooms together, but the different patterns would give each room its own identity."

"She's right. It works well in a small cottage like this."

Rounding the corner back to the central room, Maggie laid out her plans for the bookstore. "I've located bookshelves for these two walls. I'm going to keep this chair and sofa, although I'd like to have them reupholstered, and keep this coffee table. I'm also going to add another chair.

"I'm going to keep the whitewash look on the walls throughout. I think I've found curtains for this room, but I want to double check with Bree. I'd like a coordinated multicolor theme with the curtains and chairs."

Gayle imagined the room as Maggie had described it. "I like the feeling you're creating here, relaxed, comfortable, inviting."

"Come on outside," Maggie offered, leading Gayle through the back door. "I'd like to establish gardens along the fence lines, under the shrubs, and someday, when the bookstore has caught on and the weather is good, hold literary events here."

"That's a grand idea! I could contribute some pastries or a cake or something if you'd like."

"Oh yes! I'd love that!"

Returning to the kitchen to finish their tea then, Gayle told Maggie, "I love what you're planning here. I can tell you're pouring every part of yourself into your dream. You have a perfect place for it. Give it all you've got. The outcome isn't guaranteed for any of us, but I have a sense your bookstore will draw a fair number of people in."

Buoyed by Gayle's visit and assurance that whatever issues people may have had about her before were cleared up now, Maggie returned to her computer, completed the required applications and, whispering a quick prayer that she was doing the right thing, clicked to submit the forms.

Then, to keep her mind occupied and settle nerves inside her that still trembled at the thought of what she was about to undertake, Maggie turned to the list she'd developed of books she first wanted to stock in her bookstore. She selected four classics, four titles from a Dublin based best seller list, four mysteries, four romance novels, a half dozen children and young adult titles, ordering two of each book she selected with the thought that if one book sold she could order more, but if any particular book did not sell her risk would be minimized.

Maggie then turned to a list of local authors she'd developed. Choosing to wait until her business was approved and she could advertise an official opening date, she outlined a plan for inviting local artists to present their works in person, as well as a draft letter inviting local authors, one by one, when the time was right.

Anxious to see what progress had been made with the castle updates while she'd spent the week sightseeing with Maggie, Bree drove as fast as she dared to the castle grounds.

While she waited for Colleen, the receptionist, to finish with a client on the phone, Bree admired how the entrance to Allynwood was being transformed. The entryway staircase had been painted a fresh cream color, matching the stairway to the second floor whose walls had been painted the same cream, offering a bright, airy atmosphere that made the first floor feel even more grand than it had before. The reception area, whose walls had now been painted a pale mint green, carried a bright, relaxed mood and set off the fireplace in a way that made its elegant marble stand out.

"I believe Jax is tending to the rose garden outside," Colleen informed Bree once her call had ended. She pointed Bree in the direction of the door that led to the back gardens, then turned to answer another incoming call.

In all their talks about renovation, Bree and Jax had focused on interior design. Stepping outside, Bree scanned the grounds with fresh eyes, taking in gardens in various stages of cleaning and planting. Jax was working, with his back to her, trimming and cutting back rose canes to promote new growth. Despite her resolve to not let her emotions carry her too far down a path of attraction that would all too soon come to an end, the sight of his strong back and muscular arms sent her blood racing.

"You missed a spot!" Bree teased as she walked towards Jax.

Surprised to hear her voice, Jax spun around. "Hey, you're back! Did you have a good holiday?"

"It was wonderful! Grand, that's the word you would use, isn't it?"

"It is, so."

"I didn't call first to tell you I'd be stopping by. Maybe I should have."

Jax followed Bree's eyes as they scanned the t-shirt and jeans he wore, both worn through and bearing stains from soil and fertilizer. He felt a flush of heat rise up through his face, embarrassed to be caught in such shabby attire. His only way out was to make light of his appearance.

"No need to call; as you can see, I anticipated you might stop by and dressed for the occasion!"

Laughing as they went, Bree and Jax headed for the castle.

"I just thought I'd stop by and check on our progress and outline what steps we should take next."

"I think you'll be well pleased. I know I am." Catching himself, Jax added, "The owners are as well."

"Oh, are they here? You know I've been dying to meet them!" Bree quickened her pace, as if the owners were waiting for her in the sitting area or dining room.

This was it, Jax realized. This was the moment of truth, when he should reveal himself as the true owner of Allynwood. She would be put off at first, he was sure. Once he explained his reason for not telling her earlier, he hoped she would be flattered, pleased to think he was so attracted to her he feared losing her, that she was that important to him. She was not Kathleen, he reminded himself. She was a reasonable, considerate woman with no ulterior motives or designs on him he was aware of.

He owed her the truth. Bree had been open and up front with him when he asked about her background. He had not extended the same courtesy to her. She deserved better; she deserved the truth.

Jax had seen the way her eyes lit up, though, when he mentioned the owners. If he admitted to her that he was the owner, he was afraid she would hate him for his dishonesty. Fear clogged the words inside him. He could not tell her the truth.

As Bree hurried towards the castle, Jax reached for her arm to slow her down. "Whoa, Bree! Ease up there! The owners were here, but they've gone on to meet up with some friends in Dublin."

Crestfallen, Bree confided, "Are they ever here? It seems like they're always away! I'll only be here a short while longer. I do so want to meet them."

Jax still held the truth inside and hated himself all the more for continuing his deception. Instead of confessing the truth, he changed the subject. "Let me get cleaned up and I'll show you what we've got done so far."

Bree waited in the reception area while Jax washed up and changed his clothes in a workroom reserved for staff. She caught her breath when he returned ten minutes later in fresh jeans and an olive green v-neck sweater, drawn in once again by his good looks. "Hollywood would love Jax," she couldn't help thinking.

Holding her feelings in check would be harder than she thought!

Starting with the dining room, Jax showed Bree the progress that had been made to date. The pine green walls there were a vast improvement over the dark, dull walls she had first seen in that room. The worn rug had been replaced with a dark green and gold oriental style area rug she'd helped Jax locate. The oak table and chairs had been polished to a bright sheen, broken windowpanes replaced, and the windows all gleamed with recent cleaning.

The slate blue walls of the sitting room next to the dining room lent a coziness that space had lacked before, as if it now wrapped its occupants in a gentle hug. The chintz floral drapes she'd located had been hung, filling the room with a light garden feel. Cream slipcovers over the furniture were temporary; she could visualize how the sofa and chairs would look once they had been reupholstered.

"This came out even better than I imagined!" Bree saw the same pleased look on Jax. "I love how the colors flow! It will come together even more when the dining room drapes come in and the furniture here is re-covered. What do you think?"

Jax glanced around the reception area they had returned to and reconsidered the rooms they had just left. His entire face glowed as he turned to Bree and told her, "I hoped a facelift would breathe new life into this place. I never guessed it could look so wonderful."

"We still haven't addressed wall hangings or historical artifacts the owners might wish to display," Bree reminded him. "Have you been able to discuss this with them or locate any?"

Jax remembered the storage room and the photos he had still not been able to face. Maybe now, with Bree beside him, they would not be so hard to look at.

"There are some items in a storage room in the castle's cellar; would you like to go through them and see if there's anything useful?"

Bree followed Jax through a doorway behind the reception area, down a stairway, to the castle's cellar. Jax opened the storage room and flipped a switch to turn on an overhead light.

"I found a few portraits and photos here we might use."

Jax pulled pieces out one by one, careful to select none in which he appeared, focusing mainly on the original Allynwood family who were the first to own the castle. He handed items to Bree; she examined each one, setting in one place wall hangings she thought they could start with, in another photos and portraits they might consider using later on.

"This is wonderful," she told Jax when they had enough to start decorating walls with. "Could we take these upstairs, and then decide on where they might be hung?"

"I'll carry them up tonight. We can review them tomorrow if you'd like."

As they turned to leave, a sudden impulse overtook Jax. He drew Bree closer to him and kissed her, slow at first, then with more passion when she didn't pull away.

She felt so good in his arms! Her hair was soft, her perfume slightly spicy, her body firm yet yielding to his. His heart beat so fast he wondered if she could feel it between their clothes.

Bree's first impulse when Jax kissed her was to pull away. She hadn't seen the kiss coming! She didn't resist though, and soon allowed herself to respond, each of them giving in to the feelings that had been building between them. She relished being held in his strong arms, the aroma of his aftershave, the intensity his kisses carried.

Jax wished the moment could last forever. Even as he kissed Bree he prayed something would change in her life, some miracle that would convince her to stay way beyond what she had planned, maybe even forever.

Bree allowed her senses to savor every moment of passion. She couldn't remember the last time she and Carter had shared so much intimacy. Being with Jax now brought back all of how wonderful it felt to be held, kissed, loved. She wished this moment could last forever.

It couldn't though. Bree knew that. She reveled in Jax's kisses as long as she could, then gave a gentle push to separate them.

"We'd better get back upstairs. Colleen will start to wonder where you are."

"I do need to return to the gardens soon," Jax agreed. "If you're free tomorrow evening, would you join me for dinner? In the meantime, I have a folder for you of all the invoices and shipping receipts since we started the renovations; I remember you said you want to match them up with your records. Colleen has them at her reception desk; you can pick them up on your way out."

"That's fine. I'll take the folder with me and go over it all this evening. I'll have to confirm with Maggie, but I think I'd be free for dinner tomorrow."

PATRICK watched with rising anger as Gayle offered a cheery goodbye to Maggie as she departed Maggie's ... no, his ... cottage. Gayle had been on his side last he knew, understanding that Maggie posed a threat to their town, that she would have a negative impact on established businesses, that she was an outsider who didn't belong.

What the hell had happened?

He'd been away the past week, exploring job opportunities. One had been as a delivery driver in Belfast, he'd lost out on that one to a younger person who could move faster. One had been as a tour guide with a Belfast-based travel agency. He might have won that, but his temper flare up with a woman who'd cut ahead of him in line at a local coffee shop, who had turned out to be the wife of one of the travel agency partners, cost him that job. An auto shop nearby needed a mechanic; well, he had plenty of experience fixing cars, but they were older models. Interviewing for that position revealed his lack of knowledge of the computerized systems that ran today's autos. Another failed opportunity.

More desperate than ever to drive Maggie out of the cottage, he realized he would need a stronger, more sure-fire plan.

After placing her book orders, Maggie turned to the latest list of websites Liam had sent her. If she was going to name the bookstore after her ancestors, she'd better learn more about them and the region they'd grown up in.

She started reading about the Ulster Plantation, the battle for Irish independence over the British, and the 1921 partition of Ireland which created the Ireland and Northern Ireland division. When her reading led her to the Troubles, Maggie found she didn't have the heart yet to delve into that topic. Instead, she followed Liam's encouragement and studied the linen industry and how it transformed a largely undeveloped rural landscape into a burgeoning region of flax fields and drying fields.

In studying the various processes used to create linen, Maggie came to understand how the Industrial Revolution had automated and transformed the creation of linen goods, and how more modern times had moved the industry to other countries where flax was cheaper to grow and labor less expensive to create linen products.

Something was lost in the more modern approaches though, Maggie thought. She sensed a sadness for lost tradition, even though the tradition and process were hard. Back home she had always felt a sense of sadness over farm barns and silos that were left to dilapidate through time and weather, while more modern buildings took over. Here, she wished she could see fields of light blue flax flowers waving in a breeze, or watch as flax stalks were harvested, bundled for drying, processed for spinning, and then the fibrous strands woven into sheets which would become clothing or housewares. She wished she could pass by fields of linen cloth that had been washed, and washed again, and spread out on fields so the sun could bleach it.

Maggie recalled a metal sculpture she had seen in Lurgan, two figures with a linen cloth spread between them entitled the Linen Bleachers. Words had been cut into the metal "fabric", encouraging words, inspiring words. She looked now at the photos she had taken of each of the individual messages. The one that inspired her most was the one that said "believe in your dreams".

An idea struck her! She would make a photo collage of the sculpture and the individual messages! Perhaps that would inspire anyone who visited her bookstore.

AFTER dinner that evening Maggie took her cup of tea into the central room while she continued her plans, vacating the kitchen table so Bree could spread out and check receipts against itemizations on her laptop. Maggie had just started researching where Irish linen might still be made when Bree shouted, "What?"

Maggie set her laptop aside as fast as she could without dropping it and dashed into the kitchen. "What's wrong?"

"Look at this!" Bree shoved a magazine article, which had been mixed in with the invoices and receipts, at Maggie. "Read this!"

"Local Castle Undergoes Renovation." Maggie read the headline aloud. "What's wrong with that?"

"Read the whole thing!"

Maggie scanned the story which described the ongoing refurbishment of the Allynwood Castle interior, including photos of the seating area, dining room, and reception area in various stages of updating.

Maggie still missed the point.

"Here!" Bree jabbed at a sentence two paragraphs from the end of the article. "Jackson Doyle, owner of Allynwood Castle after inheriting it when his parents were killed in an accident a few years ago …".

Maggie pulled her eyes away from the print to stare at Bree, stunned. "Owner? You never told me that."

"He never told me!" Bree's rage boiled over. "So many times I told him I wanted to meet the owners before I returned home! Even today, I told him that! He never once confessed that he was the owner! He just let me go on thinking he was the handyman hired by the owners to manage the castle's upkeep!" Bree slammed her fist down on the table so hard it caused the sugar bowl, small vase and her own laptop to rattle. "Why would he do that? Why couldn't he just come out and admit he was the owner? My God, what a fool I've been!"

"You haven't been a fool, Bree. I don't know why he didn't tell you who he really was. Maybe he had a valid reason."

"Valid reason? For outright lying to me?" Tears that had gathered in Bree's eyes spilled over, racing each other down her cheeks. "I trusted him! I should have known better! After Carter made such a fool of me, after he betrayed me, I swore I'd never trust another man! How could I have let myself be so taken in by Jax?"

Maggie knew no words of comfort she could offer now would help. She spent the rest of the evening listening as Bree alternated between crying and raging, switching moods as fast as the moods of sky and ocean change when weather systems clash with each other.

Chapter Fourteen

"I have a party on the line looking for accommodations for six the second week in June." Colleen waved Jax over to her reception desk. "Will we have any rooms open then?"

"The bedrooms on the west wing will be finished next week. They can book some of those rooms. We can start taking reservations for other rooms in that wing now. We can work around guests for the updates needed in the rest of the castle." Jax stood at the welcome desk in Allynwood's updated reception area looking over a chart of the castle's available rooms. With a pencil he blocked off the rooms not yet available for booking. "Any of the rooms not blocked off can be utilized."

"Jackson Doyle!"

Jax almost dropped the chart and pencil in his hands at the angry shout of his full name. Whirling around, he found Bree, her green eyes blazing, face fire red as if she'd overused her blush makeup, waving a folder.

"Is there a problem with the invoices?"

Bree snatched the article from the folder, held it up and demanded, "Why did you lie to me? Why didn't you tell me you own this castle?"

Glancing at Colleen and a couple who had just entered to inquire about overnight stays, who were now focused on them, Jax put his hand on Bree's arm and turned her towards the entry door. "Let's go where we can talk in private."

"I don't want to talk in private! I want to know right here and now why you lied!"

"I'll talk to you outside." Jax insisted, tightening his grip on her arm. He led her to the grove of oak trees that edged the left side of the castle's lawn. Surveying the space around them, making sure they were out of anyone's earshot, he tried to explain.

"I know I haven't been honest with you. I wanted to tell you the truth but I didn't know how."

Bree shook her head vehemently, still furious, eyes piercing. "Why lie to me in the first place? Why weren't you honest right from the start?"

Jax thought back to the first time he'd seen Bree, to when her eyes, her face, her voice first captivated him. "Because I liked you the moment I saw you. I was afraid if you knew who I was you'd like me for the wrong reasons, for any fortune you might think I have, for the prestige of my owning a castle, and not for the real me."

"That's no excuse! If you liked me, starting out with a lie was a poor way to show it."

"I was in love once before!" By now Jax was pleading. "Kathleen was her name. I would have married her, but the minute she found out Allynwood was a castle with struggling finances, not a luxurious, wealthy holding, she dumped me."

Bree was too angry to feel any pity for him. "You knew my background! I told you how Carter betrayed me. I would have thought that would make a difference in how you treated me. I'd think that would make you even more careful to be honest with me."

"I should have been," Jax agreed, his face no longer stern but softer as the depth of Bree's hurt finally sank in. "I'm sorry I wasn't."

Bree stared at Jax, studying the repentance in his eyes, how the lines on his face had softened from anger to apology. For a moment his demeanor of regret almost swayed her.

Then she remembered the article, the realization that he'd lied to her not just once, but every time she asked about the owners, and her blood boiled again.

"I don't know who the real Jax is! I just know the side you've chosen to show me! How many times did I say I wanted to meet with the owners? Each time you could have confessed that it was you, yet each time you brushed the issue aside. You knew my husband lied to me, betrayed me, and how much that hurt me; but you did the same thing! I don't know you, and I don't want to!"

Thrusting the folder of invoices at him, she added, "The updates are almost done. You can handle the rest of it yourself. If you need anything, you can have Colleen call me."

With that, Bree wheeled around, returned to her car and sped off.

EVERY day, Maggie checked her mail delivery expecting her first order of books to arrive. She double checked and triple checked the delivery date the book source had listed, and checked in at the post office three days in a row only to be told each time she had no packages waiting. On the fourth day, still finding no delivery, Maggie called the company's customer service department.

"I still haven't received the books I ordered. Can you tell me when they might arrive?"

"Let me check our records." The representative on the other end of the line put Maggie's call on hold. She returned a few minutes later. "I'm sorry; our records indicate your order was delivered Wednesday last."

"Wednesday? It never arrived. I've confirmed with my post office they have no packages for me that are being held."

"We can try to trace the package if you'd like."

"How long will that take?"

"I can't say for certain, sometimes it takes several weeks."

"Several weeks?" Maggie fought to keep the desperation out of her voice. "I need those books! I'm on the verge of opening a new bookstore! I can hardly do that with no books to sell!"

Exhibiting extreme patience, the representative offered, "You can reorder the books; and if your original package turns out to have been lost through any error on our part, we can refund your original purchase price."

What choice did she have? She could not very well open a bookstore without stock. Pulling up her order, Maggie clicked on the "order again" button and resubmitted her request.

"Are you sure you don't want to stay longer?" Maggie eyed the suitcases Bree had brought from her bedroom out to the central room. "You'll be missing my bookstore opening. Don't you want to be here for that?"

Bree sat down in the chair across from Maggie and looked at her best friend. "Of course, I would love to be here to see your dream come true. It's not like I'm completely abandoning you; you can video call and text me any time so I can keep up with your progress."

Maggie nodded. "I know I can, but it won't be the same."

"I need to get home. Riley's semester is done and Regan will be home next week."

"You're running away. You know that, right?"

"I don't care! I'm done letting people walk all over me!"

"Understood. You're leaving things unresolved, though. Don't you think that will haunt you when you're back home?"

Bree repeated, "I don't care!"

After loading her suitcases into the back of their rental car, Bree turned to face Maggie's cottage. She studied it for a full two minutes, waiting until the vision her eyes beheld no longer blurred before speaking.

"It still feels surreal, doesn't it, that you'll be starting a new life here, that your dream is about to become a reality."

"It does." Maggie, as well, fought to keep emotions under control before speaking. "I'm so happy you could be here at the start of this journey. Who would have thought, when I came over to inspect and sell the cottage I'd been left, that I'd end up keeping it and moving here? I'm not sure I would have had the courage to do all this alone."

Bree slid into the passenger seat of the car, Maggie took her place behind the wheel, and they set out on the last journey they would take together for a while.

"Will Riley meet you at the airport back home?" Maggie asked as they drew near to Dublin.

"Yes. She wasn't thrilled with the idea at first, but she gave in when I threatened to take the money I would normally give her at the start of a month and use that for cab fare instead."

"That's good. I'm glad you're not going back to an empty house. Don't forget, when you get home start formulating a plan to develop your interior design business. You can use your work at the castle as a reference."

"Ask Jax for a recommendation? That won't happen!"

"Then go through Colleen. I'm sure she can work as a go between for you two. You need your work on the castle as an example of what you can do."

"Maybe." Bree didn't want to think of what she'd do once she was home. She didn't want to think of home at all. She wanted to stay in Northern Ireland with Maggie, watch her friend's business get off the ground, explore as much of Ireland and Northern Ireland as she could. For all that they'd seen, she knew they had only scratched the surface of this beautiful part of the world.

Still, in her heart she knew she had to head home. As furious as she was with him, Bree knew if she saw Jax one more time she would want him, would ignore his dishonesty, would fall deeper in love, no matter how harmful for her that might be.

They arrived at the airport. Maggie parked their car and helped Bree pull her luggage out. Then they stood beside the car, looking at each other, neither one wanting their time together to end.

Bree broke the silence at last. "Thank you for inviting me to join you on this trip! I never dreamed I'd travel this far from home. We've had quite an adventure, haven't we?"

"The best!"

Tears formed in both their eyes. In an effort to stop the moment from becoming too maudlin, Maggie gave Bree a quick hug. "You know what to do, right? You have to go through Customs, then to your gate. Have a safe flight and let me know as soon as you get home!"

Watching Bree drag her suitcases towards the Dublin airport terminal, Maggie had never felt so alone.

All while she drove back to Gaffney the shadow of loneliness rode with her, whispering in her ear how empty the cottage would be, how much she would miss Bree's company over morning breakfasts or late night wine, how now there would be no one to review the day's events with or bounce questions off of. In her mind, Maggie looked back over the years she had known Bree; she could not remember a time when she'd had a problem or challenge when she didn't discuss it with her best friend. Now who would she talk to?

As she neared her cottage, the oppressive weight of loneliness was more than she could bear. Maggie was not yet ready to enter her cottage alone. Instead, she drove to a beach she had seen in photos and placed on her wish list of destinations, hoping the scene that had looked so calming would work some kind of magic and revive her spirits.

Downhill Beach was weekday afternoon quiet with only a handful of people visible as Maggie maneuvered her car into a parking spot and walked towards the sand and water. Waves whispered in and out in gentle succession, unlike the crashing and pounding of waves she and Bree had seen at Giant's Causeway. Thankful that the wind had died down and the ocean was calm, Maggie followed the curve of the beach, absorbing the soft swishes of waves flowing back and forth, letting their quiet ways soothe her.

The few people she had seen entering the beach ahead of her were so far beyond her they appeared as walking stick figures against the swath of tan sand. On her right side the Northern Ireland coastline rose, a rugged, formidable wall. On her left, the ocean shone soft blue and silver, as if the heavens had spilled gallons of blue and silver glitter all over the water.

Solitude wrapped itself around Maggie, not like the oppressive weight she had feared as she drove towards her cottage after leaving Bree at the airport, but like a comforting hand on her shoulder, lending invisible support for whatever internal struggles she faced.

Was she strong enough to pursue her dreams without her best friend by her side? What if any unexpected complications arose? Who would she turn to if she needed a bit of comfort or support? She could always text Bree, or call her if the situation was bad enough, although the time difference would present a bit of a challenge. Gayle was just around the corner; she might lend an ear if Maggie needed someone to chat with. Gayle didn't know her well enough, though, to be able to tell Maggie when she was in the wrong, the way Bree would.

Rita would lend an ear as well, Maggie was sure. Still, like Gayle, Rita would most likely say what she thought Maggie wanted to hear, rather than give an honest assessment.

Liam might be a good source of support, or Sean McCabe, but they both had their own jobs and lives and didn't need some American woman pestering them every time she was afraid.

No, Maggie was on her own now. She'd have to find within herself the strength to handle anything that might come her way. She'd come this far in pursuing her dream. She would face the loneliness, the fear that went with it, and any other challenge that arose as she always had, head on, determined to succeed.

As she headed back to her car, Maggie picked up a seashell here, and pebble there, mementos she would place in a dish in her bedroom back at the cottage, thinking when her eyes fell upon them or when she held them in her hands they would remind her of this walk on the beach and how its soft, soothing solitude inspired strength in her.

"THANK you for picking me up," Bree said as she gave Riley a quick hug. "I'm sorry my flight was delayed; I hope that didn't interfere with any of your evening plans."

Instead of answering directly Riley told her mother, "Regan's home. We ordered pizza for dinner." She cast a sideways glance at Bree. "I know it's not what you call a proper dinner, but we aren't the cooks in our family."

Bree caught the sarcasm in the last few words Riley spoke. She chose to ignore it. She wasn't about to argue with her daughter on her first night back home.

"I thought Regan wasn't due back for another week."

"He finished his exams early."

Riley fell silent then, listening to Bree describe parts of her trip while they collected Bree's luggage, loaded it all into Riley's car, then headed home. Bree chose to let her daughter's lack of response slide as well. They would have plenty to talk about in the next few days.

"Regan! What a wonderful surprise to have you home early!"

At least Regan was more responsive, giving his mother a warm hug.

"I have so much to tell you both about!" Bree set plates and napkins on their dining room table, dished slices of pizza out, poured soft drinks for them all, then sat at the head of their table. "Wait until you see the photos of your Aunt Maggie's new cottage! She's going to turn it into a bookstore. I also have pictures of the castle I helped redecorate."

"That was your interior decorating job?" Riley cut in. "You never told me it was a castle."

"You never gave me a chance." Bree let her words sink in, then continued. "Northern Ireland and Ireland are just beautiful! I can understand why Maggie is choosing to stay there."

Neither Regan nor Riley asked questions or drew any information out of their mother regarding her trip. Bree could always read her son and daughter, could tell when they were upset or when they had something weighing on their minds. After several minutes of her running through a monologue, she gave up.

"We have all summer for me to go over photos and stories about my trip, don't we? Tell me what you're both up to!"

"We don't have all summer, Mom." Regan spoke first. "I was going to wait until tomorrow on this, but I might as well break the news to you now."

An ominous feeling rose inside Bree. "What news?"

"I just landed a job with a parks department in Colorado. My friend Andy's parents have offered me a room there for the summer so I can take the job."

"When would you start?"

"Monday." Regan watched for his mother's reaction, hoping it wouldn't be as bad as he feared.

Before Bree could respond, Riley revealed her own news. "Wendy and I want to spend the summer in Tennessee. We found an apartment we can afford, I'm pretty sure I can find a job waiting tables somewhere, and we could keep the same apartment next semester."

"All summer?" Bree was too stunned to be able to form a better response. "You'll both be gone all summer?"

"I didn't know Regan would be away."

"I thought Riley would still be home with you."

"You both thought of yourselves and not of me."

Bree's eyes had been open to a number of things during her trip with Maggie. All of those realizations clarified themselves in her mind now, the way stirred stream water in time becomes clear with sediments falling to the bottom and clean, fresh water remaining on top. Thoughts and ideas that had risen during her time away rose to the top now, allowing debris that had cluttered her mind far too long to fall away.

"That's as it should be," Bree told Regan and Riley. "You're young, you're building your futures. University is a start. Moving away and finding new jobs is the next, positive step."

"You're okay with both of us being gone?"

"Well, Regan, I won't say I'm okay with it, I had looked forward to spending time with you both this summer. The older you get the less time you'll be home; I've known this would come but didn't expect it so soon!" Bree paused, took a deep breath, then continued, "It's time for me to move ahead as well. I'm going to get a job, and I think it's time I move to a smaller place."

If she had announced she were piercing her nose and dyeing her hair neon blue, the shocked silence that greeted her would have been less deafening!

"You're moving?" Regan asked, wide eyed, when he found his voice at last.

"What will you do with the house?" Riley knew but couldn't believe what her mind told her.

"I'll sell it, of course."

"You can't!" Riley jumped up from the table they'd sat at. "You have no right to! Regan and I grew up in this house! Doesn't that mean anything to you? My God! How selfish can you be?"

"Shut up, Riley!" Regan demanded. Turning to Bree, he asked, "Couldn't you just get a job and still keep our house?"

"I suppose I could, but this house is too big for one person." Bree considered once again the rooms she had decorated, the home she had loved. "Too many memories echo through these rooms."

"I thought you treasured those memories! Now they're too painful? And if Regan and I were here, what? Would that be too painful too?"

Bree stood up, took three steps over to her daughter and fixed a firm gaze on her. "Stop this! Stop thinking about yourself! You're moving on with your life. Your brother is as well. Your father has moved on. Don't I have the same right?"

"You made our father move on! You made him so unhappy he had to get out!"

In a flash, Bree's hand shot out and slapped Riley, not a hard slap, but enough to shock them both. Riley turned to run out of the kitchen, but Regan grabbed her arm and stopped her.

"Dad didn't leave because of Mom! He left because he was a jerk!"

"Sit down, both of you." Bree waited while they both submitted, then sat down as well. "Riley, I know you're still hurt over your father's choices. We all are. He was a very good father to you both, but the truth is he was not a good husband. Oh, he provided for us, we never lacked for anything. He was not faithful, though. He had a number of affairs. I tolerated them because I thought that's what a good wife was supposed to do, stand by her husband and forgive when he strayed. Lyla was the only one of his other women who ended up pregnant. You have this image of him as a perfect father, and I don't want to spoil that image, but it's time you knew the truth.

"As for this house, when your father and I divorced I kept the house, partly because I wasn't ready to let go of it, and partly because you and your brother had gone through enough turmoil and I didn't want you to suffer any more. Every room in this house, though, carries some very painful memories for me. It's time I let go of that pain and build for myself a better, happier life."

Bree gave her son and daughter a minute to digest her words, then went on. "Before you leave next week, go through your rooms and get rid of anything you don't want anymore. We can donate things or just toss them out. Anything you want to keep, or anything you're not sure of, we can pack away in a storage unit, or take some things to whatever place I find next. Wherever I go, I'll make sure I have spare rooms for any time you come home to visit or stay a while."

Regan rose, walked over to his mom and gave her a hug. "Sounds like you know what you're doing, Mom. You're pretty amazing!" He then headed upstairs to sort his room out.

Bree received no voice of support from her daughter. Riley remained glued to her chair, staring at her empty glass.

"I'm sorry I hit you," Bree apologized. "I've never done that before, and I won't ever again. Your words really hurt me, though."

Still not looking at her mother, Riley stood up and announced, "I'm going to bed."

Regan entered Riley's room without knocking, a cardinal sin. She threw a pillow at him, he ducked and waited out her yelling at him. When her fury was spent, he sat on the chair by her desk and motioned for her to sit on the edge of her bed.

"You have to go easier on Mom," he told her.

"Don't tell me what to do!"

"I can and I will! You're not just my sister, you're my twin. I'll tell you anything I want!"

"I'm fourteen minutes older than you! I have the upper hand!"

Regan only laughed. "Whatever! Let up on Mom, will you? She's always been here for us. It's time for us to support her, whatever decisions she makes."

"But selling the house out from under us? Doesn't that upset you?"

"Why should it? We're not going to be home all summer, we'll be gone August to May for the next school year, why should she hang onto a place that makes her unhappy. You heard what she said, imagine how hard it is for her to face empty room after empty room, filled with both good and bad memories. You wouldn't want that pain day in, day out, would you?"

Riley considered her brother's words. For all that he was a torment sometimes, he was the only one who could always get through to her when no one else could. Maybe it was the twin factor; he and she were connected by a unique bond no one else shared or fully understood.

As much as she hated to admit it, Regan was right once again. "I guess it does make sense for her to sell this place. Only, doesn't it make you feel like your childhood is gone? Like, we really are becoming adults now, whether we're ready or not."

"We are adults now. It's time we stopped demanding so much from Mom and started helping her more."

"Doesn't that scare you though, the growing up I mean? What if we make mistakes, mess things up, fail big time?"

Regan wrapped his sister in a big hug. "If you fail at anything I'll always be here for you. So will Mom."

MAGGIE sat at her kitchen table, a second cup of coffee in front of her, trying to adjust to the silence of the cottage. If Bree was here they'd be chatting away, going over their plans for the day, discussing any challenges they faced, sometimes laughing over memories from the many years they had been best friends.

She wondered what Bree was doing now. Too early to call, knowing Bree would be sleeping, Maggie reached for another pastry to go with her coffee, turned her laptop on, and continued her research into some of the links Liam had provided. This led to a topic Maggie had until now avoided: the Troubles. As Maggie read story after story of one side attacking the other and the other retaliating, of buildings scarred and lives torn apart, a deep sadness enveloped her. It all seemed so senseless, so unfathomable.

Hoping Liam could help her understand the Troubles better, Maggie headed for Oxford Island, taking with her the two remaining pastries.

"You know ye need not bring any treats to try and loosen my tongue," Liam said with a laugh. "Still, I'll put the kettle on and we'll enjoy a good cuppa along with those pastries. Now, what can I be helping you with?"

"I've read more of the links you shared with me," Maggie told him as she settled herself into the chair he had pulled out for her. "I've put off reading about the Troubles until this morning. I'm not sure what to make of it, it all left me sad."

"It was a very sad time in our history. Thank God it's calmed down; I hope it remains so."

"How did it all get so out of hand?"

Liam stared out the window at the line of pale grey clouds overspreading the lough, thinking they reminded him of how the Troubles had overspread Northern Ireland. How could he explain it best? After considering several starts, he said at last, "To understand that particular time, you need to go way back in our history.

"The British overtook Ireland in the 1600s. They instituted a lot of harsh laws aimed at not only defeating the Irish, but keeping them suppressed. They also brought in people from England and Scotland to settle on lands throughout Northern Ireland. This was known as the Ulster Plantation."

"I read a bit about that," Maggie told Liam.

"What you may not have read up on is the prejudism that many of the Irish suffered during those years. The famine, in fact, was a prime example. The potato crops failed, but the rulers of that time did little to provide for the poor starving Irish, and in fact shipped Irish food products out to their colonial holdings instead of taking care of people right under their noses.

"Ireland remained under British control until 1921, when Britain gave up control of all but the six northeastern counties, which became Northern Ireland, as part of an end to the Irish fight for independence. That partition created a lot of hard feelings on both sides, and the prejudices of old carried on, leading to what was termed the Troubles. There was a great deal of discrimination against the Irish who remained in the North. Now, the Troubles have been labeled by some as a battle between Catholics and Protestants. That's oversimplifying things. It was more correctly between the Irish nationalists, many of whom happened to be Catholic, who believed Northern Ireland should still be part of Ireland proper, and the loyalists who were pro-British and largely Protestant and felt the six counties should remain under British control.

"When people have had enough of ill treatment, they fight back. That's what happened in the Troubles. Without going into who did what, who started what, who retaliated, that's the foundation of the Troubles. People on both sides were hurt, the whole region suffered."

"I wonder if prejudism is what drove my great-great-grandfather away." Maggie mused.

"Possibly. From the records I've examined, I saw he worked for a landlord who was quite kind, who did more to help his renters through the famine than most; still, others around your great-great-grandfather might very well have mistreated him and his family until he reached a breaking point. Or maybe he just grew tired of always being poor and sought his fortune in America. Whatever the case, the cottage you've inherited would have been the result of a lot of work by your ancestors in building and holding onto it over the years."

"I agree. Thank you so much for taking time to talk with me. I have a much better understanding of the history now."

"You're welcome, Maggie. Now, we've a gathering of crested grebes out on the waters today. Would you like to see them?"

As Maggie followed Liam along the trail that wound around Lough Neagh, she updated him on her progress setting up bookshelves, ordering books, eventual plans to have furniture reupholstered, and her idea of hanging photos from local artists on the walls.

"Once I get going, I also want to carry books from local authors, as you suggested, and invite them in for book signings."

"I like your ideas, Maggie," Liam told her as they rounded the end of the trail and headed back to the visitor center. "I do believe your wee bookstore will be a success."

"I hope so. Oh, I figured out a name for it; I'm going to call it Nathaniel's Place, after my great-great-grandfather."

"What a marvelous tribute! You'll do a wonderful job carrying on the heritage they've passed on to you."

THAT evening Liam returned to the home he had shared with Brigid, the home his son and daughter once filled with laughter and the odd argument or two. With Brigid and Kevin gone and Elaine moved away, the house echoed around him now.

Always, after coming back in from work, he felt the weight of silence around him. Each evening, he would heat a small dinner then settle in front of the television to watch whatever murder mystery show was on. Most nights he would fall asleep in front of the television, wake up around three a.m., force himself into his proper bed, then toss and turn until dawn.

Inspired by Maggie, in the past few weeks he had once again pulled out the set of woodworking tools Brigid had gifted him. Focusing on the craft of carving, he was starting to enjoy rather than dread his evenings. Surprised at how quickly he remembered the process of designing, making the first cuts, refining, sanding and finishing a piece, he started out small, carving a miniature duck, a dog, and a Celtic cross.

Tonight, fueled by a new idea, he hurried through dinner and set straightaway on a special project.

ON her way home, Maggie drove to Lurgan to finalize arrangements for a sign to be hung over her new business. After going over options and prices, she selected a flat wooden sign, painted ocean blue, with "Nathaniel's Place" written in bold white script, and below it in smaller letters "Bookstore".

Driving home, Maggie felt a rush of excitement. Her dream was soon to be a reality! She visualized her cottage's interior, shelves soon to be lined with books, a small fire crackling in the fireplace to soften and warm the harder edges of the room, photos to be hung on whitewashed walls, multicolor curtains adorning windows, and shades of blue, green and rose to be reflected in the rug and chair cushions and the placemats she planned to set on the kitchen table, tying the rooms together.

Maggie was so wrapped up in her vision, she didn't notice the smell of smoke when she first entered the cottage. Minutes later, as she heated water for late afternoon tea, she detected the aroma, faint at first, growing stronger as she reached the back garden.

Opening the rear door, she found the half-charred, still smoldering remains of a cardboard carton. Pouring a small amount of water at a time from the kettle she had started to heat, Maggie doused the still glowing embers, then inspected the carton's damaged contents.

The second set of books she had ordered lay in a soggy, ruined state.

This time the destruction was no accident, which led Maggie to wonder if her earlier, initial order had also been tampered with. If so, by whom? And what could she do about it?

Only one candidate came to mind, one person who would most want to see her business fail, drive her back to where she'd come from: Patrick. She had no way of proving her theory, though. She could contact the Gardai and see if they could gather any evidence, but she still moved about town with caution, concerned that some people might still harbor resentment toward her as an outsider. She couldn't afford to cause any kind of stir that would make people once again question her presence.

Only one course of action came to her mind.

"I can't help feeling Patrick's behind my lost and damaged book orders," she confided to Sean, her first step in preventing any further harm to her fledgling business. "I don't like thinking this way, but he's the only person I know of that might want me gone. Of course, there could be others . . .".

"As much as I hate to admit it, I have to agree. Patrick still complains to me whenever he can about your inheriting what he believes should be his. He still sees the cottage representing a business opportunity that could have helped him out of some financial difficulty he's landed himself in. He can't seem to find any other way out of his problems."

"I feel for Patrick, I truly do," Maggie commiserated with Sean. "I don't want to cause him any more trouble. I do need to find a way to stop him, though, if he is in fact behind the book order damage. Do you have any thoughts on how I should proceed?"

"Let me have a talk with him." Sean glanced at his calendar. "I'm off on holiday the next two weeks. I'll try to catch him before I go, and I'll let you know if I do. Don't try to contact him yourself; if we're wrong, it could make matters worse."

Maggie returned to the cottage hopeful that Sean could help sort things out with Patrick. She then proceeded to her second step: she placed a new order of books, this time with a different book supplier to save embarrassment and explanation of placing a third order with the original company. This time, instead of setting up direct delivery, she requested the order to be held at the Gaffney post office for her to pick up.

LONG after Regan and Riley had gone to bed, Bree lay awake watching lights from passing cars cast shadows across her bedroom walls and ceiling. How many nights had she lain awake watching the same light patterns, waiting for Carter to return home from work, or waiting for one or both of her children to come in from late nights out? How many times had she listened to each creak and moan of her house, heard strong winds threaten to tear shingles off her roof, heard sleet and hail assault her house's windows, felt grateful for the house's sturdy shelter? For all the many times the house had protected her, she felt she was betraying it now even thinking of listing it for sale.

Maybe Riley was right. Maybe she should keep the house a while longer, revel in its protective arms, close her mind and heart to the difficult memories. There were plenty of good memories to sustain her. Holidays dinners, kids' birthday parties, Christmas mornings, Easter basket hunts, Halloween costume constructions.

Holiday and birthday dinners when Carter failed to arrive home on time. Packing her twins off to college. Hours, days, weeks with too much time alone.

Too many nights crying herself to sleep.

No! She would not do that anymore. Clinging to a house her life had outgrown would serve no positive purpose. As she'd told Regan and Riley, she needed to close the door to her old life and start a new chapter. She was done crying, done letting fear hold her back, done worrying about what was best for everyone except her.

Maggie had shown her how to reach out and take hold of a dream. She would put Maggie's lesson to work in her own life!

The next morning, Bree made an appointment with a real estate agent to start the process of listing her house. In the next few days after that she helped Regan and Riley, when they asked for it, sorting through their possessions, letting go of some things, earmarking others for storage. She did the same with her own belongings, setting aside bags and boxes for donations, tossing what wasn't meant to be saved. She found the cleaning process cathartic, letting go of fears and painful memories with each new box she packed.

The night before they left for their summer adventures, Bree took Regan and Riley out for dinner at their favorite restaurant, allowing Regan to order their best steak, and Riley the lobster dinner she so loved.

"I'd like to thank you both," she started out after their dinners had been ordered. "You did what I asked in sorting your rooms out. I know it wasn't easy for you."

"I know our being gone this summer isn't what you planned," Regan answered. "Thank you for understanding and giving us both the freedom to do what we want."

Riley fixed her most serious look on her mother. "Mom, I know I've treated you pretty bad lately. You were right, I was the selfish one. And I didn't mean what I said about you being responsible for Dad leaving. Well, I meant it at the time, but you showed me I was wrong. I am so sorry."

Bree reached across the table to give her daughter's hand a tight squeeze. To both of her twins she said, "I can't believe how grown up you are. I'm so proud of the people you're becoming. No matter where I end up moving to, no matter what happens next in my life, I'll always be here for you both."

Chapter Fifteen

Maggie couldn't say why, but two days before her bookstore was set to open she woke up to visions of her mother. Not ghostly apparitions floating in the air around her, but visuals as clear as day rising and falling, appearing then fading. Each new image carried memories of times with her mother, some happy, some sad, many laced with tension as she and her mother hit myriad rough spots in their relationship.

Images of her mother made Maggie think of Ohio, of the home she was leaving behind, and of the friends and acquaintances she would now rarely, if ever, see.

A cloud of sadness overshadowed her as she moved through her morning. As she stacked books on shelves and rearranged plates and cups on her kitchen counter, she found her hands trembling the slightest bit and nerves tied her stomach in knots.

Not one to take huge risks before, Maggie was now embarking on the biggest risk of her life. And why not? Her mother was gone, Maggie was no longer tied to her care or the preservation of a relationship that was at best an arm's length dance of circling around each other's feelings.

Her job had been terminated; that was no longer the safety net it had once been. She had no students to introduce to the great masters of literature, no youthful creative writing talents to nurture.

True, she could have stayed in Ohio and sought a new teaching position, and perhaps in time would have found one.

An unexpected gift had interceded, an inheritance calling from a foreign land she belonged to even though at the time she had not known this.

Now, as she finished her work and stepped back to survey the arrangements she had completed, she felt for the first time she truly belonged in this place.

An incoming phone call interrupted her thoughts.

"Maggie, it's Liam. Are you free this afternoon?"

"I could be, why?"

"The sun is out, the wind is calm, and I have someplace I'd like to show you."

Half an hour later Liam picked Maggie up. He wouldn't tell her where they were going, only that it was someplace exciting.

As they rode past green rolling hills and an occasional glimpse of blue water, Maggie felt a connection deep in her soul to the landscape they passed. That landscape was part of her story, part of her heritage. When Liam stopped at the Magheracross Viewpoint and Maggie looked out on its magnificent views of the Antrim coastline and the ocean's vast expanse, she realized she did not feel as much like a foreigner, but more like someone who had a kinship with the ground she stood on and the beauty spread out before her.

"This is stunning," Maggie told Liam, her voice hushed, in awe of the grandeur before her.

"It is, but it's not the surprise place I want to take you, just a warmup."

Liam headed east along a coastal route that took Maggie past Dunluce Castle and Giant's Causeway, places she and Bree had visited, places Maggie had promised herself she'd return to. Liam did not pull into any of those sites, though, but instead proceeded along a road that afforded Maggie more views of the ocean and the countryside along the Antrim coast.

As she rode along, Maggie was even more aware that she no longer felt like a tourist taking in views that would live inside her long after she returned home. She was home.

Liam pulled into the parking lot at a spot Maggie was equally intrigued by and afraid of, the Carrick-a-Rede Rope Bridge.

"I'm not sure I'm ready for this," Maggie told Liam, hesitating to get out of the car.

"You are," he assured her. "I'll be with you every step of the way."

The walk from the car park to the bridge took them along the coast. Maggie noted the water's colors varied from brilliant blue to greenish and to an aqua she had only seen in photos of the Caribbean. Maggie could see the bridge in the distance and tried to suppress the fear that rose inside her. She would not let Liam see how afraid she was.

As they crested the hill the walkway led over, Maggie could see stairs leading down the side of a cliff to the rope bridge.

"You didn't tell me I had to go down a cliff!" She moaned, stopping in her tracks.

Liam gave a light laugh. "Some things are best left for a surprise! So far no one's slipped into the waters below; you'll be fine."

"I don't know if I'm ready for this."

"You're not going to quit now, are you?"

Maggie watched as people ahead of them managed the stairs and the bridge with ease. It didn't look too deadly. And she was no quitter. With a deep breath, Maggie turned to Liam.

"I'll do this if you go ahead of me."

The stairs turned out to be not as bad as they seemed, and Maggie soon found herself walking across the steel and wood bridge suspended between the cliff and the edge of a small island. From the island, Maggie could see color depths and cliffside views she never would have noticed from the mainland.

"Wow. This is more incredible than I ever would have imagined!"

"There's a reason I wanted you to do this today," Liam told her. "The weather's perfect, no rain or wind to make you even more reluctant to cross the bridge. More than that, though, you mentioned last week you were nervous about the bookstore, about making such major changes as moving here and leaving your prior life behind."

Pausing to study the bridge a moment, Liam asked, "How do you feel now you're on the other side of the bridge?"

Maggie took stock of her feelings before answering. "I've overcome something I was a bit afraid of. I feel quite proud of myself!"

"Does that give you more confidence that you'll succeed in this new life you're building?"

Studying the stairs along the cliffside and the bridge suspended over water and rocks, recalling the jubilance she felt when she reached the island's solid ground, a sense of triumph built up inside her. "I think so," she told Liam. "You showed me how to push past my fear here. The bridge has pretty solid supports that make it safe. As long as I have support from you, and from Gayle and others I've met in Gaffney, I do believe I'll be fine."

THE day before her bookstore was set to open, Maggie inspected every inch of her setup. She wiped the kitchen counters clean for the twentieth time, making sure no fresh dust had settled, admiring all over again how the clear tea mugs and small plates set next to the electric kettle shone in morning light entering in through the window over the sink. She adjusted each of the four wooden chairs that surrounded their matching kitchen table, making sure each chair was straight and equidistant from the table and from each other. Stepping into the cottage's central room, she dusted for the dozenth time the edges of each bookshelf as well as the mantel over the fireplace and the low central table upon which she'd placed a Northern Ireland photo book she had found online. She inspected the books on each shelf, eyeing their lineups, making sure each row was straight, admiring the variety of colors and print as each book's spine faced out for easy identification to browsers. She repositioned the two easy chairs opposite the fireplace, then stepped back to survey their positioning and the overall balance of the room.

It felt right. The colorful book spines blended with the soft colors woven into chair fabric that coordinated with the area rug under the coffee table. The gleam of the mantel's copper candlesticks mirrored the gleam of the kitchen area's counters, tabletop, and clear dishes. The green and blue hues of the landscape photos she'd hung on the cottage's white walls drew out the shades of green and blue in book spines and fabric, tying the room together. The atmosphere the rooms presented felt relaxed and inviting, enticing all who entered to browse at their leisure, enjoy a cup of tea and perhaps a piece of shortbread, Maggie's specialty, and consider the purchases they might wish to make.

It all felt so right.

Come evening Maggie would bake shortbread, filling the cottage with its irresistible aroma. Now, though, she would run to the florist in Lurgan, pick up a bouquet to add color to the kitchen table, then stop into the coffee shop for what she guessed would be her last relaxing afternoon for a while.

At the florist shop Maggie bought two bouquets, rose and field flower combinations in pink, white, red and lavender shades. She then drove back to Gaffney, left one bouquet in her car to place in a vase once she returned to her cottage; the second she brought into the café and handed to Gayle.

"This is for you, just a little thank you for all the support and help you've given me."

"Maggie, these are lovely! You didn't need to give me anything, though."

"I know I didn't have to, but I wanted to. Your friendship and support have been invaluable to me."

Gayle poured a fresh cup of tea, set a chocolate biscuit on a plate, and pushed them both towards Maggie. "On the house," she insisted, waving away Maggie's motion to pay.

"Thank you. You know I'm addicted to these biscuits!"

"Are you all set for your grand day tomorrow?"

"I am. I can't believe my dream is coming true."

"You've worked hard for this."

"You'll stop by tomorrow, won't you?"

Gayle smiled, nodding yes. "As soon as my morning rush is over. I want to check out what kind of competition your shortbread will be!"

While savoring her tea and biscuit, Maggie pulled out her phone and reviewed the checklist she'd developed of all the tasks she had to take care of before her bookstore's grand opening. With each task she was able to check off as completed, her smile grew wider and the inner tension she'd carried eased a bit more.

MAGGIE had just left the café and returned to her car when a text from Bree came through.

"Can I ask a favor? Could you contact Jax on my behalf and see if he can provide a recommendation for me that would help me land an interior decorator position here?"

Maggie read the text from Bree three times, each time formulating a different response. Why don't you contact him directly? Hooray, you're finally going after your dream! Of course I'll contact him.

Instead of texting any of these responses back, Maggie called Bree.

"I know I could have texted, but I wanted to hear your voice. I miss you!"

"I miss you too."

"Do you have any leads yet on interior design jobs? Or are you just preparing yourself in advance?"

"Preparing in advance." Maggie heard Bree take a sip of coffee then set her mug down. "I know I don't have the degree or experience necessary, but I'm hoping to get a foot in the door somewhere as an apprentice or assistant while I pursue a degree."

"You mentioned last week you were considering selling your house. Are you still thinking about that?"

"Yes. When I told Regan and Riley they were upset at first, you know, selling the home they grew up in and all that. Then they realized they're moving on with their lives and I need to do the same. Which leads me to a second favor I'd like to ask of you."

"Whatever it is, you know I'll say yes."

"I already have a couple interested in buying my house. They're coming in from Maryland and they're pushing for a quick sale. If I haven't found a new place by the time they close on my house, is there any way I could move into your condo just until I sort out a new place for myself?"

"Of course! That's a brilliant idea! In fact, why don't you just go ahead and buy my place. We can work out all the details. With three bedrooms there you'd have plenty of space for when the twins are home or when I come back for a visit."

"I was hoping you'd say that!" Bree's excitement carried clearly across the phone line. "Are you sure you're okay with that?"

"Okay? I'm thrilled with the idea!"

"Maggie, you're the best!"

"I'm not as great as you think. I know you want me to contact Jax to ask about a referral. I could do that, but I think it would be better coming straight from you. You worked with him, not me, and I'm sure he'd like to hear from you."

"I can't. Oh Maggie, I was such a fool to even start to have feelings for him; then when I found out he lied to me …". Bree paused, Maggie guessed to wipe away tears and regain control over her emotions. "I wouldn't take his calls before I left. It's hard enough needing a reference from him now; I don't have the courage to call him directly."

"I think if you called him you'd find talking with him easier than you imagine. Still, if you'd rather I'll reach out to him this afternoon."

DECIDING a personal visit was a better way to approach Jax than by telephone, Maggie drove out to Allynwood Castle within an hour of her conversation with Bree.

The Jax she met with appeared with circles under his eyes and a haunted, brooding look behind them.

"Maggie, it's good to see you." Jax set down the hammer he'd been using to drive nails into walls so the portraits and photos he and Bree had chosen could be hung, and offered Maggie his hand.

Maggie accepted his handshake and gazed around her. "Wow! If I hadn't seen Allynwood before, I would not have believed such a transformation could happen so quickly!"

"It's all down to Bree." Jax hesitated. "I haven't heard anything from her. Did she make it home okay?"

"She did. In fact, she's why I'm here."

Panic flashed across Jax's face. "She's not hurt is she? Is she okay?"

"Bree's fine. She's starting to look for interior decorating work back home.

She asked if I would contact you and see if you'd be willing to provide some kind of recommendation regarding her work here."

"Of course I would." Jax looked crestfallen. "She couldn't bring herself to reach out to me on her own?"

Maggie felt for the man before her, realizing his feelings for Bree ran far deeper than she had imagined. She debated whether the next truth should be spoken, deciding it had to. "Bree's divorce hit her hard, the past few years she lost any confidence she had, any ideas or dreams of what she could do once her son and daughter entered college. Her working here was the first time she started to believe in herself, and others, since then. She trusted in you. That was a big step for her, after her husband had so badly betrayed her. You really hurt her."

Jax looked even more haunted. "I didn't mean to. I've tried to apologize but she won't take my calls."

Maggie found it impossible to stay mad at the man before her laid low by the heavy load of guilt and sadness he carried. Her heart softened a degree. "Start with the referral. Perhaps write a message to go along with it. You can send both directly to her or provide them to me and I'll pass them along."

A glimmer of hope rose across Jax's face. "Yes, I'll do that. Thanks!"

Returning to the cottage, Maggie was surprised to find the front door open a crack. "I was sure I locked this!" She spoke out loud as she stepped inside.

Her purse and the bouquet of flowers she'd carried fell to the floor as she surveyed the scene before her, trying to make sense of what she saw.

Photos had been removed from walls and smashed against the hardwood floor. Books, yanked off their shelves, lay strewn all over the room where they'd been dropped or thrown, some of them with pages ripped out and tossed about. Black aerosol paint left ugly swaths across curtains, chairs, and walls. In the kitchen, black paint marred the surface of the now overturned table and ruined the counters and cabinets. The clear mugs and plates Maggie had taken such care with had been shattered, leaving broken shards scattered across the floor.

Unable to comprehend why anyone would have trashed all she'd worked so hard to build up, Maggie at first tried to gather up picture frames and photos, and as many of the undamaged books as she could to set them back in order. The task was too great though, and the damage too extensive.

Too shocked and heartbroken to be angry, she sank onto one of the armchairs and cried.

Chapter Sixteen

"Grand opening postponed until further notice"

Behind the sign, behind the cottage's locked door, Gayle and Liam did their best to console Maggie.

"Did you call the Gardai then?" Gayle asked as she hung dark towels across the cottage's front windows to prevent people from looking in.

"Yes, they've been here and gone, before I called you two."

"Did they say anything about what they thought happened?"

"No, Liam. They could tell the lock had been forced open, they searched for fingerprints or forensics, but it looks as if whoever did this was professional, wore gloves, left no clues behind."

Tears blurred Maggie's vision again as she surveyed the central room. "I can replace the books, but what am I going to do about all the black? How do I get that out? And what if whoever did this comes back? Is it ever going to stop?"

"It will," Gayle assured her. "You might not see that the Gardai found any evidence, but they may still have picked up clues we aren't aware of."

"There's a product we've used at the nature reserve to remove spray paint vandals have left graffiti with a few times," Liam told Maggie. "I can get some for us, and we'll clean what we can of the paint. Anything we can't get out we'll find a way to hide."

Maggie rose from her chair, wiped her tears away, and turned to her friends. "Thank you, both of you, for being so supportive. I knew calling you was the right thing to do. Alright! If I'm going to turn this nightmare around, I'd better get started!"

"I'll put the kettle on," Gayle offered.

"Let me run out and get the paint cleaner," Liam suggested. "I'll be back soon and bring some sandwiches as well."

While Liam was gone, Gayle and Maggie cleaned up what they could of the damage that had been done. Broken glass was gathered and thrown into a refuse bin, and the floor was swept clean of any remaining fragments. Books were gathered and inspected for damage; the ones that could not be saved joined the glass shards in the refuse bin.

Liam returned with enough paint removal solvent to clean the cottage three times over. "I know it's a lot," he admitted, "but I've found it sometimes takes more than I anticipate. I didn't want us running out."

Starting with the kitchen counter and table, they applied the cleaner, allowed it to set a few minutes, then scrubbed it off. When café work and Oxford Island duties called Gayle and Liam away, Maggie continued, taking short breaks when the work overwhelmed her and fresh tears rose in her eyes.

Every afternoon Bree called to check on Maggie's progress. When she'd first heard about the delay in the bookstore opening, her initial thought was to fly over and help her best friend out. Maggie talked her out of it.

"You have enough on your plate with selling your house and looking for a new job. I'd rather have you back here for a visit when both our lives are a bit more settled."

By the third day, the kitchen counter and table had been restored to their pre-damage state, and Maggie had decided the cupboards needed repainting to fully conceal the black stains.

"I'll find some banners to hang on each for now," she told Gayle and Liam. "That should hide the marks I couldn't get out."

As they continued to work, Gayle asked, "Have you heard any more from the Gardai?"

"No, not yet."

"You and I both know who's responsible." Gayle watched for Maggie's reaction. "This has all the indications of something Patrick would do."

"Who's Patrick?"

Maggie looked at Liam, then Gayle, then Liam again. "The relative I've mentioned who thought he should have inherited this place instead of me."

"Has he given you trouble before? Do the Gardai know this?"

Gayle explained to Liam, "Ever since Maggie came here, Patrick's been trying to force her to give up this place and go back home." She turned to Maggie. "You do need to tell the Gardai the other things he's done to you."

"They did ask if I knew of anyone who might want to have a go at me," Maggie admitted, "and I did mention Patrick, but if they have no evidence there's not much they can do. Pointing a finger at him might make things worse if there's no proof he was involved."

Liam remained quiet while Gayle and Maggie traded comments on whether Patrick was to blame, how to handle him going forward, and when Maggie's grand opening might be rescheduled. After Gayle left for the night, though, he sat across from Maggie at her kitchen table and spoke up.

"I've no right to offer an opinion on this, you and Gayle are more directly involved and familiar with Patrick. Still, I have a thought you might want to consider."

Maggie smiled. "You have as much right as anyone, Liam. You've become a good friend; I respect anything you have to say."

Liam spoke with care, weighing his words to balance his concerns for all involved.

"I've never met this Patrick, but it sounds like he could conceivably strike again, is that right?"

"Yes, it's been a bone of contention on his end, he feels he was cheated out of what should have been his."

Liam nodded. "Did you not also say he's met with some hard times recently?"

"Sean, the solicitor I work with who also knows Patrick very well told me that."

"Right. I just wondered, isn't there some way to help Patrick turn his life around a bit? Then he might not be so inclined to take vengeance out on you."

Maggie hadn't considered this before. "That's an interesting thought. I'm not sure what I could offer, though."

"No, you couldn't, you're straining your resources as it is opening your bookstore which, I might add, is very lovely, or will be once the damage is fully repaired. Nor could the help come from you. We Irish have a fierce pride inside us! He would not accept your help, I'm quite sure. Still, you know the history. We've talked about it several times; you've done an excellent job with your research. Your ancestors built this cottage at a time of great hardship. One of your kin is facing hardship now. Might there be a way to honor your ancestors by helping one of your relatives now?"

Maggie considered Liam's words. "You're right. I'm naming my bookstore after my great-great-grandfather, Nathaniel. That might please him, but he might be even more pleased if I could find a way to help Patrick, in a roundabout way, of course, so Patrick would be more receptive."

"Maggie, you're a wise woman. Now, settle yourself in for the night and get some rest. I'll be back tomorrow afternoon, after my duties at the nature reserve are completed."

"I'll have the kettle ready, and dinner if you'd like. I made some beef stew yesterday; there's still a fair amount left."

MAGGIE spent a long while considering Liam's suggestion. By the next morning, an idea had formed in her mind.

Her first step in putting her plan into action was stopping by Sean McCabe's office. "You know my bookstore was vandalized the other day. I suspect Patrick was behind it, although I can't prove it at this time."

Sean agreed. "It sounds like something Patrick might do."

"I have two choices. I could have the police initiate formal charges against him. Or I could try to find a way to help him."

Raising his eyebrows, Sean told her, "I've known Patrick a long time. No one else has been able to turn his life in a good direction, not even me. I'm not sure you can succeed where others have failed, but what did you have in mind?"

"Before I tell you my plan, let me ask you: what do you think Patrick wants more? To own the cottage? Or to have a job that provides a steady income and something he can point to with pride?"

"That's a fair question. If I had to choose between the two, I'd have to guess it's the steady income he would want more."

"I was hoping you'd say that." Maggie whispered a silent prayer that her idea might work, then told Sean, "What if I could find a job he might like? I have someone I can reach out to who might be able to offer Patrick a job. I could have this person contact Patrick directly or contact him through you so it doesn't look like it came from me, you know, preserve Patrick's pride and all. Do you think that might give Patrick enough of a reason to drop his plotting to drive me out of the cottage?"

Sean didn't answer right away. He thought on Maggie's proposal so long she was sure he would say it was a terrible idea, it would never work. When he responded at last that it was a good idea, Maggie whispered a prayer of thanks.

"Great! Let me make a call or two. I'll get back to you."

MAGGIE'S next call was to Jax. "I have a favor to ask."

Jax was glad to hear from Maggie. If he had a line of communication open with her, he had a chance to connect with Bree. It might take a long time, but he was willing to wait. "If I can help with anything, I'd be glad to."

"I know you do as much of the work at the castle as you can. I know someone who needs a job, though; I wondered if you had any openings, any job you might be able to offer him."

"I'm sure I could find something. Do you know what qualifications he has, what kind of job he's looking for?"

"No, I'm sorry. I can't ask him, he can't know I'm involved with this. It's hard to explain. I can put you in touch with someone who would know."

"I'd be glad to help if I can. Now that the first round of renovations is complete, we're taking more reservations and I'm busier than ever. I don't have time to handle everything the way I had before. Hiring someone to help would make sense."

Maggie gave Jax Sean's phone number. "I'd appreciate anything you can do."

Before she had a chance to hang up, Jax told her, "I sent Bree a referral, but I'm not sure if she received it. Can I send one to you that you can forward to her?"

"Of course." Maggie felt bad for him. She understood Bree's silence, knew all Bree had gone through and how deeply Jax's dishonesty hurt her. Still, Jax seemed to be doing everything he could to make amends. She hoped Bree would at least break down and respond to his phone calls or messages. Not communicating at all would resolve nothing.

"I'll make sure she gets your referral," Maggie promised.

She couldn't resist. Before sending Jax's referral on to Bree, Maggie read it. In it, she found such glowing praise for the work Bree had done that Bree could not possibly continue to hang onto her anger towards him. She forwarded the referral to Bree, hoping it would not only help her friend find a job in the interior decorating field, but also reestablish communication between Bree and Jax.

Then she called Bree. "Hey, just wanted to let you know I've emailed Jax's referral to you."

"Thanks so much." Bree hesitated a moment then asked, "How is he?"

"The truth? He's still devastated you haven't been in touch with him."

Bree pictured Jax as she had last seen him, embarrassed that he had been caught in his lies, pained that Bree was walking, no running, away from him. Part of her was glad he was still hurting.

Part of her, buried below layers of her own hurt, admitted that she missed Jax, that she was still drawn to him.

Turning her laptop on, Bree checked her e-mails. She saw several messages from Jax, and one, just received from Maggie. She opened that one first.

The referral Jax sent gave more high praise for Bree's work than she felt she deserved. He complimented her talent for developing color schemes, for combining old and new, and for staying within budget while locating fabrics, accent pieces, and contacts who could handle upholstering and other services needed. He emphasized her accessibility and pleasantness to work with, concluding with the words, "highly recommend for any interior decorating position".

Next, Bree opened the latest e-mail Jax had sent. Along with the same referral Maggie had forwarded, Jax had written a personal note. She read that now.

"Bree, I want to apologize one more time for the hurt I have caused you. I never intended to cause you pain. In trying to protect myself, I failed to consider how my actions might impact you. I realize you don't want to be in contact with me; I will stop reaching out to you, but if you ever do wish to talk, please know I would welcome that."

Jax was passing the ball off to her. Any next move would have to come from her.

What, then, did she want to do?

After reading Jax's referral and cover message, Bree decided to read the other messages she'd been ignoring. With each message, her desire to see Jax again and discuss all that happened between them increased. Leaving things in the stalemate they were at now would do neither of them any good.

Regan and Riley were settling into their new environs. The apartment Riley and Wendy were sharing looked safe and adequate, and Riley had already lined up a summertime job at a local coffee shop. Regan and Andy had already settled into Andy's parents' home and were working as well.

Her house sale was confirmed. True, Bree had a lot of packing to do, but half of what she had she was willing to let go of. One massive moving sale a couple of weeks before closing should clear a lot of remaining things out. Maggie had already started sorting the paperwork to have Bree take over her condo; with the spare key Maggie had given her years ago, Bree had gone over several times, messaged with Maggie to determine what items Maggie wanted stored away, what furniture Bree could let go of, and what items could be shifted to a spare bedroom so Bree could start settling herself there.

If she booked a quick trip to Ireland, she could take a run up to Allynwood and work a few things out with Jax, surprise Maggie at the bookstore's rescheduled opening, and still be home with plenty of time to finalize packing, moving, and closing on her house.

AFTER three or four phone calls between Jax and Sean, a plan was formulated. Sean called Patrick into his office and laid the plan out.

"You're responsible for all the vandalism at Maggie's bookstore. I know it, you know it, and the Gardai know it."

Patrick started to protest, "I never …", but Sean held a hand up to stop him. "We have proof. Now, you have two options. Either Maggie presses charges and you go to prison, or you accept the job proposal I'm about to give you."

Patrick still pushed back. "You can't force me. I haven't done anything wrong."

Sean never lost his temper with a client or friend but came close to it now. "Patrick, we can prove you've been involved. Ever since Maggie inherited the cottage you've tried to force her to give it up and go home so you could claim the cottage for yourself. For what? You didn't care about the cottage, just about the money you could make off it. For years you've complained about the hard times life has given you. You want to make money? Here's your last chance. The owner of Allynwood Castle is looking to hire a property manager. The person he hires would work directly under him and be responsible for maintaining the grounds and the building. He's willing to pay a good salary.

"Now, you either take this offer, take responsibility for turning your life around, and swear on an affidavit I have prepared and will keep here in my files that you will leave Maggie and her bookstore alone for the rest of your life, or I will defend Maggie's charges against you and you'll be sent down."

Patrick stared hard at the man seated across from him, his counselor, the man he considered a friend. He didn't seem like a friend today. Patrick wondered how Sean or anyone else could prove he'd been behind any of the damage at Maggie's place; he'd been so careful to not leave any evidence or trace of his presence behind. Sean must have something, though, or he wouldn't be so confident now.

Patrick could call his bluff, demand Sean prove whatever evidence he had. Or he could take the job regardless. After all, what he'd wanted all along was a way to make money, either income from turning the cottage into a bed and breakfast or selling the place outright. Property manager at a castle? The title sounded impressive! And a castle was bound to pay well.

Let Maggie have her cottage, he decided. She wasn't worth facing a stint in prison. He signed the papers Sean set before him, including an employment agreement confirming he would start at Allynwood Castle the next day, and left looking forward to his future rather than backwards to all the disappointments and failures he'd carried so long.

Jax met with Patrick, assessed his attitude, mannerisms, and willingness to take on any and all aspects of the property manager position, and knew he'd made the right choice. He worked with Patrick to develop a schedule for the next phase of plantings and improvements of the garden along the stone wall to the left of the castle grounds, as well as a list of the next round of updates inside the castle.

Maggie sent a card thanking Jax for helping her out, along with a gift card to be used at her bookstore and an invitation to the rescheduled opening. He should be thanking her instead, he thought. Patrick was not only a hard worker, his abilities with a paintbrush and a masonry trowel were equally impressive. Allynwood looked more and more like a classy, well-appointed castle people would not only enjoy, but would want to return to time and time again. Already, glowing reviews had started appearing on various travel booking websites, and potential developers had stopped bothering him.

Jax received an e-mail from Bree thanking him for the referral and wishing him well with Allynwood's remaining improvements. He wished he could show her in person how things were shaping up. At least he could send photos, he thought, and keep some kind of communication with her open. It was better than closing the door between them forever.

The evening before Maggie's bookstore's rescheduled grand opening was set to take place, Liam stopped by with fresh flowers.

"What a lovely surprise!" Maggie invited him in and motioned to one of the chairs. "Have a seat. Would you like some tea?"

"Thank you, that would be nice." He ran his hands over the slipcovers Gayle had donated as a temporary solution for the marred upholstery. "Your bookstore has come together very well, young Maggie."

"Now that Patrick has a steady income and a job he loves, from the reports I've received, I don't think I'll have any more problems."

Liam accepted the cup of tea Maggie handed him, but didn't sip it. Not normally one to be at a loss for words, he found he had trouble speaking now. He reached into his jacket pocket, pulled out a tissue wrapped item, and set it before Maggie.

"You inspired me to return to a hobby I loved but had drifted away from. Thank you. This is for you."

Stunned, Maggie turned the gift over in her hands a couple of times before opening it. Removing the tissue paper with care, she soon held a wood carved replica of her cottage.

"Liam! Oh my gosh! This is beautiful!"

"Do you really like it?"

"Are you kidding? It's amazing! Oh, you even carved Nathaniel's Place over the front door! Liam, I can't believe you made this!"

Pleased that she liked his gift, he told Maggie, "I hope this little replica will remind you of me. You'll be busy now. I shall miss seeing you at Oxford Island, or coming over to help now your bookstore is sorted."

An unexpected sadness filled Maggie's heart as well. "I'll find time here and there to visit you, and you're always welcome to stop by."

Having expressed the first level of his feelings, Liam took another chance. "If I asked you to dinner some evening, would you join me?"

Maggie tried to downplay her feelings, but inside her heart a warm glow spread. "I would like that."

Chapter Seventeen

Bree could hardly contain herself as she hurried through Customs, dashed to the car rental counter at the Dublin airport, and headed for Northern Ireland and Allynwood Castle.

Soon she would know if what she'd felt for Jax was just a fleeting romance or something more real.

Excitement and fear combined within her and grew stronger with each passing mile. By the time Allynwood's entranceway appeared, her stomach competed with the ocean's waves for tossing around. The wheels on Bree's rental car kicked up stones as she hurried into a parking spot, threw open the car door, and dashed up Allynwood's entrance into the reception area.

"Where is he?"

Stunned, Colleen didn't answer right away. When she recovered from the surprise of seeing Bree, she took a defensive stand. "Are you here to cause trouble?"

"No!" Bree forced herself to calm down. "I just need to talk with him, Colleen. I promise I don't want to cause a scene."

"Your leaving really hurt him. I don't want to see him hurt again."

Tears rose in Bree's eyes. "I don't want to hurt him anymore. Please, Colleen, tell me where he is."

Relenting, Colleen pointed outside. "He's working on the rose garden."

Bree could not get outdoors fast enough!

"Jax!"

Wheeling around, Jax found Bree running towards him. He dropped the clippers he'd been using to trim rose canes, and ran to her.

"Bree! What are you doing here?"

"I had to see you! Jax, I was wrong to leave you the way I did! I should have discussed things with you instead of just running off."

"No, it was my fault! I should have been honest with you right from the start. I was wrong to lie to you the way I did."

Bree scanned the grounds, saw the wrought iron table and chairs they had once occupied was free, and motioned towards them. "Can we sit down and talk?"

They took their places at the table, then Bree spoke.

"First, thank you for the recommendation you gave me. I think you might have exaggerated my abilities just a bit, but I do appreciate your words. I have no doubt what you wrote will help me advance my career."

"I didn't exaggerate at all," Jax told her. "You did excellent work."

"Whatever!" Bree almost laughed. "Anyway, that's just part of why I came back." Measuring her words with great care now, Bree told Jax, "I found myself drawn to you, Jax. I told myself not to; we're from two separate worlds, there's no future for us.

"Maybe I'm wrong though. If what I felt for you is real, and if there's any chance you feel the same way, maybe we should explore things further."

"Maybe we should!" Jax rose, drew Bree up from her chair, wrapped his arms around her and kissed her long and slowly. Abandoning the rose garden, he strolled Allynwood's grounds with her, pointing out improvements he and Patrick had started to address, stopping at several points along the way to kiss Bree again.

MAGGIE sat at the table she'd set up in the small garden at the back of her cottage. Fairy lights twinkled among the branches of the oak tree that stood in the back left corner and the holly and azalea shrubs that anchored the garden's rear right corner, while overhead stars competed with the fairy lights for attention.

While the rest of the town around her settled in for the night, she sipped her glass of champagne and reviewed the day's events.

The grand opening of Nathaniel's Place bookstore went so much better than she'd hoped. With most traces of the vandalism removed, thanks in large part to Liam and the product he provided to remove the black spray paint stains, and Gayle's slipcovers that rescued the damaged upholstery that still needed replacing, the central room and kitchen area shone, warm and inviting to all who entered.

And enter they did!

Gayle appeared at nine when Maggie first unlocked the door, bearing a plate of her best pastries. "I know you have shortbread ready, but I thought you might like to offer these as well!"

Gayle browsed the shelves of books, found a romance novel that appealed to her and purchased it, promising, "I'll be back later, after the café closes. Good luck!"

Rita from the corner market stopped by before her work shift and bought a novel for herself and a children's book for her young granddaughter. "You've a lovely place here, Maggie! I hope you do well."

A steady stream of customers kept Maggie busy throughout the day, some complimenting her on her selection of books, a few relaxing in her chairs while enjoying a cup of tea and a pastry or shortbread treat, a few she could tell were just curious about the newest business in the area.

Bree texted her in the morning wishing her success. She was not prepared when, an hour before closing, Bree stepped through the front door, accompanied by Jax.

"What?" Maggie was stunned and confused! "What are you doing here?"

"Only giving my best friend the support I should have given her weeks ago!" Bree hugged Maggie, then stepped back and surveyed the rooms around her. "You've finished this all so beautifully, Maggie. I'm so proud of you."

That evening, after the bookstore closed and Liam, Gayle, Bree and Jax joined Maggie in celebrating with a small light dinner, Bree related her afternoon visit to Allynwood.

"I wanted to surprise you, but first I wanted to clear the air with Jax. Maggie, I needed to see him. I had to find out for myself if the attraction I felt for Jax was just a vacation romance, or something more real."

"What did you discover?"

Bree couldn't hide her happiness. "I really do like him, Maggie. We talked a lot of things over. I know he's not Carter, that his hiding the truth of his identity wasn't sinister. I know it's not who Jax is inside. I don't know if we'll be able to maintain a long-distance relationship, but we both agreed we need to give it a try."

Watching Jax and Bree now as they strolled around the garden, Maggie sensed the attraction between them was strong. Maybe, she thought, her best friend would live close to her again.

Maggie was met with another surprise that day when Sean and Patrick entered her bookstore.

"You've done an amazing job with this place," Sean told her. "Your ancestors would be proud."

"They would, so." Patrick added. "Maggie, can I have a word with you in private?"

That was the only part of the day when Maggie felt uncomfortable. Still, with plenty of people milling around Maggie guessed even if Patrick tried anything all she'd have to do was call out and any number of people would rush in to help.

"Okay. We can step into the kitchen to talk."

Out of earshot of the others, Patrick coughed to clear his throat, then told her, "Maggie, I'm sorry I gave you so much trouble. I never intended …". Here Patrick stopped, cleared his throat again, and continued, "I was jealous. I had plans for this cottage that I couldn't let go of. My life was falling apart around me, I thought this place would be my lifeline. Thanks to you, I have a better outlook, a good job and hope for my future."

"I'm glad things are turning around for you, but it's not down to me."

Patrick sent a knowing look Maggie's way. "I know Jax is a friend of yours. I can add two and two. I just wanted to apologize and say thank you."

Maggie smiled back at him. "I'm glad you stopped by. I hope you'll come back sometime."

After Sean and Patrick left, Liam told Maggie, "You've done a remarkable job, not just with the bookstore and restoration of the cottage, but also with the way you've helped Patrick out. Your ancestors would be proud of you."

Now Maggie sat at the table, admiring the glow of fairy lights throughout her small garden, Bree and Jax, Gayle and Liam seated around her, all of them finishing what was left of the champagne Liam had brought along with cheese and crackers and assorted appetizers. She was aware of the chatter around her, but she didn't join in, at least not for a while.

Her mind was centuries away.

She thought of her father, Hugh, a man she had never known, who had never forgotten her. She thought of Susan, her mother, who had tried her best to raise her daughter alone. As imperfect as her parents may have been, they had given her life; and her father, with the inheritance he'd left her, had given her a new life, one she never expected but now could not imagine missing out on.

Someday Maggie would explain to Liam how, that night, she could feel the presence of others, invisible yet without a doubt there. As sure as she felt her own breath, she felt theirs. She swore she could hear whispers, or a sense of others talking, some in an ancient tongue she had yet to learn. Even though she could not decipher the words, a feeling came over her she was a thousand percent sure of: Nathaniel McCarey and all her ancestors were pleased with all she had done and were bestowing their blessings upon her.

Acknowledgments

Writing and releasing any book requires a lot of support from those around us. I am grateful to my sisters, Laurie Roeser, Maureen Walek, and Roberta Sendker for always supporting my endeavors. My aunts, Ann Crisafulli and Ann Meister, have also always encouraged me, and I am grateful to them.

Beth Bales Ostrowski, our 2012 Ireland adventure was just a small part of the fun we have shared. Your gift of friendship is one of the best blessings in my life.

Fr. Jerome Kopec, your encouragement to embark on my 2016 solo Ireland trip also played a huge part in writing this book. Thank you.

Michael and Marian Davis, our 2023 Irish adventure added to my knowledge of and sense of Ireland and Northern Ireland and helped to inspire this book.

Joyce Grinewich, thank you so much for reading this manuscript and pointing out what needed improvement. You and Bob Grinewich are such wonderful sources of support and encouragement, and I am grateful always for you.

My thanks also to a wide circle of friends. I hesitate to name friends as I don't wish to leave anyone out, but I do wish to recognize Charlene Rosati, Kim Krajewski, Linda Morgan, Dave Delaney, Patrick Hulsman, Terry Doughty Cathel, Danica Horner, Derek and Amy Mungons, Dave and Sandy Reid.

Tom McDonnell at Dog Ears Bookstore and Kristine Sutton at Newstead Public Library, I am grateful for your continued support.

Mark Pogodzinski at NFB Publishing, none of my books would exist without your hard work. Thank you, as always.

Don Stoll, every day you support, encourage, and inspire me. I am most grateful for your presence in my life.

www.ingramcontent.com/pod-product-compliance
Lightning Source LLC
LaVergne TN
LVHW021236080526
838199LV00088B/4546